healing
his MEDIC

First Published in Great Britain in 2018 by
LOVE AFRICA PRESS
103 Reaver House, 12 East Street, Epsom KT19 9EY
www.loveafricapress.com

ISBN: 978-1-9164755-0-2
Also available as an ebook

PRAISE FOR NANA PRAH

Praise for Path to Passion

"Path to Passion is a journey with a bit of mystery and suspense, some snarky humor and smexy times all wrapped up in heartfelt romance. I highly recommend it. " ~ Felicia Denise

"Exciting and captivating." ~ Maya Love

Praise for A Perfect Caress

"Ms. Prah did a wonderful job bringing the atmosphere and ambience of Italy to life and I will admit they were among my favorite scenes in the book." ~ Debbie Christiana

"Sweet and fun and passionate." ~ Love Bites and Silk

Praise for the Destiny Series
" Incredibly addictive and soaring with heat." ~ Lucii Grubb

"Beautiful writing, fabulous character development, and hot and steamy love scenes! I love it!" ~ Stephanie Sakal

" Nana is entertaining and thought-provoking." ~Diana Wilder

ALSO BY NANA PRAH

Destiny Series

Midwife to Destiny

Destiny Mine

Entwined Destiny

Destiny Awakened

The Astacios

A Perfect Caress

Path to Passion

Ambitious Seduction

Others

Love Undercover

Love Through Time

This book is dedicated to all readers of romance novels set in Africa. May you never run out of excellent books to entertain you.

CHAPTER ONE

The dead weight of Navy Commander Akin Solarin's naval brother in his arms didn't keep him from running towards the hospital. Despite the strain in his legs and the burn in his chest, he didn't stop for one second. Ishaq Obatola had squeezed himself into a tight ball, moaning in agony while they'd been sailing on the dinghy from their destroyer, *Reckoning*. Akin's own stomach had clenched with sympathetic pain and worry. Such moaning couldn't spell anything minor.

Waiting for a helicopter to reach their ship for an emergency transport would've wasted critical hours. When they had landed on the shores of The Gambia, they'd ordered a taxi to get them to the hospital with great haste.

Bursting through the doors of the Emergency Room, Akin spotted an empty stretcher and lay his friend onto it. Ishaq groaned as he rolled onto his side and tucked his knees to his chest.

"We need help. Help us!" he bellowed.

The four other officers who'd escorted them off the ship looked around the empty space and joined in the call, pushing open doors in search of someone. Anyone.

A woman came running through a pair of double doors that one of his men had yelled into. Her gaze darted around the room in alarm. Once they fell on the man curled up on the stretcher, she propelled into motion, reaching for a gown from a shelf and slipping it on in the few steps it took to reach them. "What happened?"

Did it matter? His best friend was in agony. Taking a breath, Akin drew on logic. "He said he's been feeling unwell and complained of severe pain in the lower part of his abdomen. On the ship, he said it might be his appendix and insisted that he had plenty of time before he'd have to see a doctor."

As the medic put on a mask with a plastic shield attached, two more hospital workers arrived. A pair of gloves completed the first woman's outfit before she rushed to the stretcher, where she placed two fingers along the side of Ishaq's neck. "What's his name?"

"Ishaq Obatola."

"Mr. Obatola, can you hear me?"

Without opening his eyes, he groaned before mumbling, "Appendix."

"That's for us to determine. Let's roll him into the examination room," she said in a crisp British accent that meant business.

Akin followed the squeaky stretcher through the swinging doors into a semi-private room. "It's *Doctor* Obatola."

The woman snapped her gaze up to Akin. "A medical doctor?"

He nodded. "Yes. So he should know what he's talking about."

"Dr. Obatola, I need you to lie on your back for me," the woman coaxed.

He could only presume her to be the doctor from the way she'd taken control and everyone else deferred to her.

She and another fully protected worker helped Ishaq onto his back while someone else took his temperature and blood pressure. Akin admired their ability to work as a tight-knit team.

Her fingers hovered over Ishaq's belly. "I'm going to palpate your abdomen."

Ishaq tried to draw his legs up in an attempt to prevent the woman from touching his belly. He drew in a breath before opening his lids to look at the doctor with bloodshot eyes. "Right lower quadrant pain," he mumbled.

"The rebound tenderness will make me pass out," he added after a deep grunt. "I'll give up my license if it isn't an appendicitis. It hit me too fast. Ultrasound, no time for X-ray. Surgery."

He then closed his eyes, his breaths harsh and fast.

The doctor considered him for a moment before turning her head to one of her staff. "Sara, please bring the ultrasound machine."

Akin's heart slowed its pounding as his esteem of her went up. She'd decided to listen to her patient rather than her ego.

"Blood pressure is ninety over sixty, pulse one-twenty, respirations forty. Temp is thirty-nine," the only male attending to Ishaq read out as he wrote on a paper.

The person she'd sent for the ultrasound came sliding to a halt with the equipment.

The doctor set up the machine. "I'm going to need you to lie flat so I can scan you."

Ishaq swallowed hard, and with a strength Akin admired, did as she asked. Clenched fists and jaw were the only signs his friend showed of being in pain as the doctor did her work.

She spoke directly to Ishaq when the grey picture came on the screen. "We're taking you to surgery, Dr. Obatola. You're abdomen is filled with fluid."

"Burst."

"Yes, your appendix has ruptured. Monica, alert the surgical team of an emergency appendectomy. Tariq, draw blood for a complete blood count, type, cross and match."

Akin gripped the edge of the trolley as terror squeezed the air out of his chest. He'd prefer taking out a slew of enemies in battle rather than seeing someone he considered a brother die.

The doctor touched Akin's shoulder. Warmth and a tingle made its way along his arm.

"We'll take good care of him."

Her reassuring grin alleviated a fraction of his trepidation. The awareness of her as more than a medical personnel did not.

CHAPTER TWO

Exhausted, with eyes too gritty to keep open without effort, and sipping on lukewarm coffee, Doctor Comfort Djan stepped into the long hallway. Her walk towards the testosterone-crowded waiting room set her belly quivering. The overpowering presence of the men had weighed on her as they'd watched her every move in the Emergency Room.

The surgery she'd assisted Dr. Peters with had taken hours longer than expected. She'd heard of doctors not taking care of themselves—hell, she could plead guilty—but she didn't think it was the case with her patient. Things had gone wrong for him too quickly to control.

She didn't look forward to updating the group of Dr. Obatola's condition. She should've opted to review the patients for Dr. Peters instead.

Hovering outside the door of the waiting room, she assessed the group. She'd never considered a man in a military uniform sexy, but these guys made her reconsider. Each stood as a mountain on his own, but the one she'd spoken to in the Emergency Room snagged her attention. Everything about him screamed leader. Guardian.

From his intense deep brown eyes, which complimented his golden skin, to his broad chin. She'd noticed the flare of his upturned nostrils when he'd heard something he didn't like. His firm lips had stayed pressed together as he'd given a curt nod when he'd been told that his friend had to be rushed to the operating room.

As if sensing her, the man raised his head and went from seated to standing at a height of what had to be six-foot-two in one lithe movement. The others followed.

She walked up to him, attempting to stay just far enough away so she wouldn't have to crane her neck in order to glance past the darkened shadow of stubble covering his strong jaw and into his expectant eyes.

Flanked by his men, she mentally reinforced that this was her domain, not theirs. "Mr..."

Had she learned his name? No.

"Akin."

"Mr. Akin—"

"No, just Akin. How is he?"

She clasped her hands in front of her and squeezed. "Dr. Obatola made it through the surgery."

The collective sigh of relief warmed the air.

She held up a hand to provide the rest of her news. "Not only had the appendix ruptured, but he had a diffuse infection of the peritoneum. When—"

"You just operated on the only man among us who could've understood what you just said."

Akin's scowl disturbed her. How could such a handsome face look so frighteningly reprimanding?

"Can you please speak English?" he continued.

She could do without his harsh tone, but the request was acceptable. "A small structure of his intestine burst open, and the inner lining of his abdomen was infected."

She scrunched her nose as she remembered the offensive smell which had gushed into the operating room when they'd cut him open.

"We normally make a small incision to remove the appendix." She held her thumb and pointer finger about four inches apart. "The incision we made is much bigger because we needed to clean out his abdomen. He has a tube connected to a bulb in place to drain out the fluid. Depending on the amount of drainage he has overnight, we'll see if we can remove it tomorrow."

She dragged her gaze away from Akin's and focused on the friendliest-looking of the four. "We have him on pain medication and antibiotics. He's resting comfortably."

"Can we see him?" the friendly-looking one asked, with a crooked grin.

"Yes, but only for a short while."

"Thank you, Dr..." Akin looked down at her chest. Her hardening nipples didn't understand that he'd only searched for her nametag. "Djan."

"I'll show you the way."

Or she could direct them there so she'd be out of their presence. When had her body ever reacted to a man just looking at her before?

It must be the fatigue.

Akin had never experienced such a rush of lightheaded relief as when he saw Ishaq. How could a dark-skinned man look pale? It was a wonder his best friend hadn't died.

"I'm going to kick your ass, just as soon as the doctor gives the okay to do so. Why the hell did you wait so long? You're a damn doctor."

Ishaq's eyes crept open with a groan. "I'm on my deathbed, and you're yelling at me? What kind of brother are you?"

"One you scared the hell out of," Akin answered. "She said they had to gut you and clean out all of your shit, but you'll be fine."

Ishaq's smile was small, but present. A good sign. "I'm sure that's exactly how she expressed it."

"She left out the shit part," Dubem said. "But we knew what she meant."

Ishaq responded with a grunt as his eyes closed.

Akin took a moment to send up a gruff prayer of gratitude. God hadn't featured much in his life, but he couldn't deny His presence during times like this.

They stepped away from the bed to let their brother rest.

Dubem rubbed his hands together. "Now that I know he's okay, there's a fine honey I'd like to talk up."

Commander Dubem Nzeogwu had the reputation of getting any woman he lusted after with little more than a flash of his double dimples and a few sweet words. Did he want to make a play on Dr. Djan? Akin's short nails dug into the flesh of his palms.

They'd made it to the door when the soft patter of feet caught his attention. The woman who'd helped save Ishaq's life swept into the room with a nod and an antiseptic scent. She went to their comrade and spoke in soft tones Akin couldn't discern. He turned his full attention towards her, unable to keep his eyes from roaming along the lushness of a body that even a baggy light green uniform couldn't hide.

Dubem's low whistle made it to Akin's ears.

For the first time in a very long time, a deep stab of jealousy twisted in his gut, and he restrained himself from punching the pretty boy in the jaw. "Don't even try it."

Dubem's eyes narrowed for a flash. Akin got the impression that he'd been seen as a rival the man hadn't expected.

Dubem raised both hands up in defence and laughed, distilling the tension that had crept between them. "Fine."

Dr. Djan glanced in their direction. Akin's heart stilled for an incredible moment as their gazes met. Her obsidian eyes held his as he soaked in the flawlessness of her dark skin. The scar reaching upward from her eyebrow to the hairline intrigued him. What had caused it?

He'd probably never know.

The corners of her lips rose into a slight smile as she focused on her patient again. Yes, her beauty had captivated him, but the innate sorrow he'd witnessed in her irises tore at his spirit. Screaming at him to bring her peace. What could've happened in her life that had caused her eyes to be filled with such agony and despair? It had registered earlier, but he'd blamed the observation on his own anxiety.

"Akin," Dubem said.

"What?"

"They don't like it when you stare."

At the sound of Dubem's chuckle, Akin forced himself to look away to glare at his friend.

The laughter continued. "Just a bit of advice. With your *charming* personality, you'll need all the help you can get."

Akin knew the truth when he heard it. Unless the woman liked direct, forthright men who couldn't stay in one location to save his life, he had no chance.

CHAPTER THREE

Comfort snapped the curtain closed around her patient and willed her heart to slow. A doctor with trembling hands couldn't be trusted. Akin made her nervous. She'd felt him searching for something when their eyes had met. Probing where he had no right to be.

Why had she volunteered to check on the patient for Dr. Peters? She should be in her room struggling to fall sleep. Not working five hours of overtime. And yet, she'd stayed.

She smiled down at Ishaq after a brief examination. The man barely fit in the bed.

Akin's feet would've hung off the edge if he'd been lying in it.

Why did that man feature in every thought she'd had since meeting him?

"You're going to be all right, Dr. Obatola."

"Thanks. Please call me Ishaq. After all, you just saved my life."

She raised her brows. "Actually, that was my colleague, Dr. Peters. He's on staff at this hospital. I'm a guest with *Médecins Sans Frontières*."

The nod had his eyes drifting closed. "Doctors Without Borders. I hope my negligence didn't endanger my people."

"No, you should all be fine. The hospital had its last newly reported case of Ebola about a month ago."

Three weeks ago had marked the last death from the Ebola outbreak around this region. She held her tongue. Grim news of the little boy who had hung on while the rest of his family had died wasn't necessary to share with someone who'd just barely escaped death himself.

"Ebola is a bastard," Ishaq grumbled.

"You get no argument from me."

When Comfort pulled the curtain back, she expected the room to be empty. She however met the piercing gaze of the man who had the ability to make her blush. What was it about him?

Power. She'd recognized it right away when she'd first encountered him. He possessed a raw virility. A devastating sense of authority.

Still, that had never registered with her before. At least, not in this manner.

"Have a good night," she said when she could get her mind to kick in.

"I'll walk you out," the most approachable of the group said.

Where had he come from? It had only been Akin in the room, hadn't it?

Did Akin just growl? She gave him a second look and glanced quickly away from the scowl he shot his friend's way.

"It's okay..." she started, but she didn't know his name.

The man tilted his head, and two adorable dimples popped out on his dark-skinned cheeks when he smiled.

"Dubem Nzeogwu." He winked. "Dubem will do. The rules on your posters say there's no unnecessary touching. Otherwise, I'd hug you for saving our friend's life."

Such a charming man. And handsome, too, with those high cheekbones and long lashes framing angled eyes. Yet, he didn't appeal to her like Akin.

"Dr. Peters performed the surgery, and I assisted."

"You observed the severity of the situation and sent him to the operating theatre right away," Dubem said. "If I've learned anything from Ishaq, it's that a good doctor knows when to get help."

She smiled. How could she not when she was genuinely pleased by his words.

Dubem touched a hand to his chest. "And you're beautiful, too. Your smile alone must've healed millions."

Was Akin part bear, because the sound coming from his throat was meant to threaten.

In her teens, she would've fallen for such a line. Her thirties had brought more discernment. "Thank you. I still have a report to write. Have a good night."

As if she'd acquired a parasite, Dubem followed her. "No worries. Akin can stay with Ishaq for a moment while I walk you to your office. To be honest, I think he's ready to throw me through a wall. We've been together all day."

His stage-whisper would've allowed Akin to hear him.

"Oh."

What more could she say? Akin didn't seem the type to tolerate nonsense, while Dubem with his flirtatious style used frivolity to his advantage. Might as well save the hospital from having to plaster a wall with a human-shaped hole through it. She allowed him to walk with her.

Dubem shook his head. "It's been a trying day. First, we take down a pirate ship. Peacefully this time, but there's always those moments of uncertainty. Will they or won't they fight."

Comfort's neck snapped back. "Did you say pirate ship?"

"Yes. It's the work we do. Why we had to bring Ishaq here, of all places. Don't mind Akin, he's normally nicer than this."

The man had her head spinning with this conversation. What did Akin's behaviour have to do with pirates?

The truth spilled from her lips. "Somehow, I don't believe you."

Dubem chuckled. "Okay, so nice isn't the right word. How about cordial?"

They really shouldn't be gossiping.

"Less growly would do," she added.

"And you'd be right on point. He's a good guy. Just a little rough."

She waited for him to finish the sentence. When they'd reached her destination seconds later and he hadn't, she contributed, "Around the edges?"

Brows scrunching together and lips pursed, he shook his head with vehemence.

"No. He's rough through and through." Then, the jovial man laughed once again. "I'll send him to you. I think you would make great friends. Of course, not as good as you and..." He let the sentence hang.

What the hell? Where had that come from? Before she could pull her thoughts together, he winked and turned to return to Ishaq's room.

With the long hours she'd worked that day, maybe she'd misunderstood.

Comfort entered the room she'd been using to assess clients for the past couple of weeks. Since the passing of their last patient with Ebola, they hadn't admitted anyone else with signs of the condition. MSF was still being cautious and keeping their staff on the ground. Not one to sit idle, she'd taken up the role of a consulting doctor.

The hospital was happy to have her. It felt good to treat people who weren't at an extreme risk of certain death.

Making her way around the desk, bone tired, she plopped onto the chair with a heavy sigh before sliding Ishaq's folder towards her. If she put the paperwork off until tomorrow, she'd still have to do it. Might as well get the dreaded aspect of her work completed. Head down, she focused on writing the report so she could finally get some rest.

She finished the last couple of sentences before raising her head at an unexpected knock and blinked several times. What was he doing there?

"How may I help you, Akin?"

"Dubem just remembered that you said you wanted to see me."

She didn't mind admiring the fine man, but she'd never called for him. She scratched her temple. Or had she? And then, she recalled Dubem's parting words.

She could at least be gracious. "Please have a seat."

He eased himself into the chair without his bulk breaking it.

Picking up a pen, she wiggled it between her fingers. Realizing her jittery action, she put it down and clasped her hands together. Comfort forced herself to look into his amazing chocolate brown eyes. "I didn't call you here."

He cocked his head in a moment of confusion before narrowing his eyes and baring his teeth. "I'm going to kill him. And then, you can revive him so I don't lose my job."

She bit her cheek to hold in her laughter.

"He came up with the idea that we'd make good friends. I have no idea where he got such an impression." She leaned forward as if she'd found a conspirator to confide in. "His ideas flittered from one to the other with no supposed connection. Does he have any psychological problems?"

Akin burst out with a rusty-sounding laugh that had her wanting to grab her stethoscope to listen to his lungs. Since when did laughter sound painful?

"No, Dr. Djan. Unlike a few of our other crew members who could be considered borderline, he's mentally capable. Just a little high-strung when he's not engrossed in his work. He has a tendency to be excessively flirtatious when women are around, but he's a good man. One of the best I know."

"Sounds like a high recommendation."

He nodded. "It is. Although I can say the same for the majority of the men on the ship."

She raised an eyebrow. "The men you capture pirates with?"

"We're a specialty navy crew. The best of the best." His voice rang with pride as he puffed out his chest.

Their uniforms had told of their naval status, but she was curious about the specialty aspect. He hadn't called themselves Marines, so who were they?

"Must be why you're a little wobbly on land."

He angled his head. "Pardon me?"

"Sorry, little army joke at the expense of the navy. I was in the British army reserves."

A twinkle lit his eyes.

"I served during my college and medical school years." She would've gone in full time after completing her education if tragedy hadn't struck, leaving her debilitated. She tapped her chest as her heart squeezed in pain at the memory. With a deep breath, she attempted to control it. "Which country do you belong to?"

"Nigeria."

So she hadn't impressed him enough to take them beyond curt answers. Rough wasn't a good enough description for him.

"What's your rank?" She'd pin money on him being a captain.

"Commander."

Close enough. If this alpha was a second in line, then she'd hate to see what the captain of the ship was like.

Her mind flashed back to the emergency room. "Two of your people spoke with a French lilt in their African accent."

"How could you hear? You were busy saving a life."

"I'm a former army reservist and a medical doctor. Nothing much gets past me." Maybe he'd loosen his tongue now.

"I see."

Perhaps not. Might as well appease her curiosity. "Are you working on a Nigerian vessel?"

"No. We work for WASPA. West African Sea Protection Alliance. An organization which defends the Gulf of Guinea from pirates and others involved in nefarious activity."

She shook her head. "According to the news, they've become more prominent and violent over the years."

He nodded as the down-turn of his lips returned. "This is why the West African countries have banded together in an attempt to stop them."

"And how's it going?"

He sat up straight. Was frowning his most natural expression?

"The Gulf of Guinea is a large territory for one ship to cover. I can't reveal the exact statistics of our monitoring and interventions, but our presence is better than none at all."

Incredulous, she angled her head, unable to stop a brow from rising. "You happened to be closest to The Gambia where there's been an outbreak of Ebola. You all took a great risk stepping into this hospital."

He pressed his lips together. "We had no choice. It would've taken the helicopter too long to get to us before flying us to a safer hospital. Ishaq could've been dead by then."

He leaned back into the seat. She wasn't fooled by his more relaxed posture. The man always seemed to be ready for action.

"Besides, the news said there hasn't been a new case in the entire country for the past month."

"Still risky."

He shrugged. "It was either that or watch Ishaq die. No option."

A heaviness settled into her. She completely understood. Inevitable death without action versus possible viral haemorrhaging illness and later death. "Looks like the virus is in remission."

Akin shook his head, and the chair creaked under him. "Such a travesty. So much suffering."

What could she add to the astute assessment? She'd seen it all first hand and still couldn't believe the amount of anguish it had caused.

He stood, and she did the same. Time for her to go home.

His towering frame attempted to intimidate her as she rounded the desk.

"How long will Ishaq be admitted?"

Her back straightened in defence at his dark expression and gruff tone. What the hell had she done now? *Be a professional.* "We'll have to see. The surgeon will let you know tomorrow."

"You won't be here?" Alarm tinged his voice.

The Goliath confused her more by the minute. Why should he care if she showed up or not? Other than when she'd mentioned being in the reserves, his demeanour hadn't been friendly. *Rough.* Like the shadowed stubble on his cheeks. Would the short hairs abrade her lips if she rubbed them against him? Or would the hair and beautiful golden-brown skin be soft against her needy mouth?

She blinked herself out of the fantasy. "I'll be around. The surgeon will be the one to discharge him."

Akin rubbed the back of his neck. If she knew him better, she'd swear he'd become uneasy. He possessed too much confidence to ever show his nervousness.

"Are you working through the night?"

"No. My shift ended a while ago. I need to get some rest for tomorrow." *If the demons will leave me alone enough to sleep.* "Are you going back to your boat?"

She couldn't help using the most offensive word someone could say to a navy sailor.

"Ship."

She laughed at his immediate correction. The small joke would never get old.

He responded with a smile that snatched her breath from her throat. The small gesture of full pinkish-brown lips stretching to expose bright teeth took the man to a higher level of gorgeousness than she could endure. She looked down the corridor.

"I'll be staying at the hospital tonight."

They'd reached Ishaq's room. She wouldn't concern herself with where Akin would rest his head. She'd known military who could sleep while standing.

"I'll walk you to your place."

The offer set her off balance as she stood on the spot. A gentleman. Not what she'd expected. "It's okay. I don't stay far."

He glared down at her with a furrowed brow. Couldn't he stop trying to control everything for a moment?

"I'll walk you there," he stated.

The bubbling giddiness in her stomach prevented her from arguing. She liked being with him. Maybe if they had more time, they could be friends. Perhaps Dubem possessed complete sanity, after all. She liked Akin's straight to the point manner. In a world where people told you what they thought you needed to hear, he was a refreshing experience.

She didn't consider the silence between them amiable. Yet, it didn't make her want to increase her pace, either. She'd have to analyse it when she struggled to fall asleep later.

The walk to the hospital quarters where she shared a room with one of the MSF nurses took all of five minutes. The request that she always be paired in a room with someone had been questioned, but eventually granted for all of her tours with MSF. The role of being ever present during the night, which her ex-husband had naturally played, would be assigned to strangers. She wouldn't have been able to join them if she'd had to endure sleeping in a room alone. Her past haunted her too intimately.

She waved a hand at the single story, painted cement structure where the MSF staff assigned to the hospital were housed. "We're here. Have a good night."

He reached out and touched her arm. The electrical shock she'd experienced the first time she'd touched him had returned.

"Doctor."

She raised her gaze to his. In the external light, his eyes had darkened to a inky shade which held her captivated.

"Yes."

Why did her voice sound breathy? And even worse, how come she felt the need to step forward and have him wrap those massive arms around her? Security. Peace. Affection. Things she'd been missing for a long time.

"Thank you for saving my friend's life," Akin said. "Have a good night."

Before she could respond, he turned and headed back to the hospital.

It took a moment for Comfort to regain control of her legs and move from the spot. Tomorrow, she'd avoid seeing him at all cost, even if right then, she wanted to chase him down to discover more.

What would be the point? Navy didn't tend to settle down. The one military man she'd dated back in college had tried to control every aspect of her life all while secretly dating three other women. Not a situation she ever wanted to face again.

Her family had helped her handle the situation. Their support had always been immeasurable.

Her family. She swallowed hard to push down the pain. They were the reason she'd taken a job that whisked her all over the world. Even if she couldn't claim happiness, her work with MSF distracted her.

Maybe one day, time would've healed her, and she'd feel that soul-deep joy of life that had been stolen from her.

A quick glance over her shoulder revealed Akin's easy stride disappearing into the darkness. Or maybe not.

CHAPTER FOUR

A hospital was no place for a person to get quality sleep.

Akin stretched his neck from side to side to ease the kinks which had developed from sleeping in a chair at his friend's bedside. He'd refused to leave Ishaq and had sent the others back to the ship.

The night had been filled with disruptive activities of the nurses checking on their patients and giving medication.

Fantasies of the beautiful doctor with her perfect dark brown skin, intense eyes, and full lips had pervaded his mind all night. He'd replayed their conversation and her expressions. Why hadn't he spoken more? Maybe complimented her or used the miniscule amount of charm he possessed. Granted, he'd been himself, but he'd wanted to grab her attention. In a positive way. Make her take an interest in him. Being gruff and monosyllabic as was his nature when he engaged with strangers had more irritated her than impressed.

Her stint as a reservist, even if it had been in the army, had raised his respect for her. As if it had had anywhere to go—she'd helped to save his friend's life.

Comfort emitted a sweetness he couldn't resist. Yet, a gloom hovered within her. One he'd give anything to release.

He shook his head. What about her had affected him so deeply? His heart had stirred as a familiarity had flowed between them while attraction raged. A sensation he could use more of.

It didn't matter. Just like everyone else he'd ever been involved with, she'd eventually leave him if they got together. An inevitability. He wouldn't give up the navy. Couldn't. The sea had claimed his heart long before any woman had attempted the venture.

One of his sailors walked into the room, targeting him. James reached him and saluted. Akin returned the gesture. Although the crew came from the various countries of West Africa, they'd discovered early who outranked whom. It led to a well-organized ship.

The man from Cape Verde stood at ease. "Captain wants you back. He sent me to relieve you."

Akin hid his disappointment at not being able to talk to the enchanting doctor again. He nodded acknowledgement and stood by Ishaq's bedside. "I'll see you back on board."

Ishaq looked at him with bleary, reddened eyes. At least, he looked better than he had yesterday when he'd been curled up in the foetal position. Unspoken emotion ran between them. Soul brothers didn't need words to understand each other.

Akin swallowed hard. "Don't harass the staff."

Ishaq laughed. "I'm the least of their troubles."

"What? You hold the record for being a horrible patient. It's a wonder the crew didn't throw you overboard that time you came down with malaria. Miserable SOB."

"If I'd been taking the pain medications back then that they've put me on now, I would've been much better behaved."

"I've got to get going. Captain waits for no one."

Fighting the urge to search for Dr. Djan, if only to see her one last time, Akin strode out into the cool, salt-tinged air. The sea beckoned, and as always, he'd answer.

Akin headed to the bridge as soon he'd stepped onto *Reckoning*, their mighty destroyer. "Where's the captain?"

"In his office."

For a moment, he contemplated heading towards his own cabin to wash off the grime he'd acquired last night. One of the men had returned and dropped off fresh clothes and food, carting away his uniform. He'd washed up as best he could in the bathroom, but it couldn't replace a shower. He set off to see the captain.

The steel panel made a dull reverberating sound when he knocked.

"Come in."

Entering, he located his leader at his desk, saluted, and stood at attention.

"Have a seat."

In the course of Akin's twenty-year service in the navy, Captain Emmanuel Obot registered as the most powerful person he'd ever worked with. Not a big man in stature, he'd actually just made the height cut-off to enter the navy. But his strategic intelligence couldn't be surpassed.

"I received the report you sent with the men last night. It's good to hear Ishaq pulled through."

Akin held back a grin knowing his friend would live. "He looked even better this morning."

"He's a good man," Captain admitted. "Like the rest of the crew. Handpicked as the best by their superiors. The ship will feel the loss of his retirement."

Akin could only nod. He was still trying to convince his friend to stay in the navy. So far, Ishaq had adamantly declined, claiming the need to be with his wife and children on a permanent basis.

Akin's retirement date would pass with him still being on the ship. He aimed to one day become a captain, and nothing would stop him.

Someone knocked on the door.

"Enter," Captain said.

Dubem came in, saluted, and sat at the captain's nod. Dubem and the others had left for the ship when Akin had returned to Ishaq's room. He could've choked the man one-handed last night for setting him up like he had. Never mind that it had given him the chance to talk to one of the most fascinating women he'd ever met—he didn't appreciate being manipulated.

The captain's chair squeaked as he shifted to lean his elbows on the desk. "I was just about to brief Akin."

"Yes, sir."

What was going on? A briefing with only the Executive Officer and the Captain meant a major issue had arisen. What could they have in store for him? He schooled his features to maintain a neutral expression.

"Early this morning, I spoke to the doctor who operated on Ishaq. He'll be out of full-time commission for a few weeks." Captain Obot paused. "It's imperative to complete this tour. Governments have spent millions on this project, and we need to ensure its success. Not just for us, but the safety of the ships leaving West African ports."

Why was he preaching at him? Akin knew all of this. "We're heading back to Lagos."

He presumed they were. They'd make a full sweep as they returned, apprehending any illicit activities they encountered. Waiting a couple of days until Ishaq was well enough to board wouldn't alter things too much.

The captain gave a curt nod. "This afternoon. By order of the council of West African admirals."

Akin clenched his jaw. "Are they aware that our doctor is in the hospital after having nearly died?"

His senior officer's thinned lips and single sharp nod revealed how much he disliked the order.

"They are." He glanced through some papers piled on his desk. Pulling one out, he held it up. "Due to the danger of our work, we can't sail without a medical doctor. Here's their solution."

Akin stole a quick glance in Dubem's direction before reaching for the sheet. His friend must already know the details although his stony expression didn't indicate that he was happy about it.

It didn't take long to read the letter. Even less time to reject every word of it as ridiculous and too perilous to adhere to. He laid the paper on the desk instead of shredding it. Her life would be at stake. Didn't they understand?

Akin's heavy sigh of frustration expanded his nostrils. What could he do? Even if he argued against it, in the end, the order must be implemented. The navy wasn't a democracy. Once an edict had been issued, it was expected to be followed. He'd never had a problem with it before.

Right then, his instincts insisted that he fight. "Their solution will give us more problems."

Not that he believed Comfort would agree to the proposal.

Captain Obot's expression was unreadable as he retrieved the letter, folded it along the existing creases, and placed it in an envelope before handing it to Akin. "Admiral Omehia contacted *Médecins Sans Frontières* who spoke with the administrators of the hospital to have Dr. Comfort Djan released from their service. She has accepted the position. She'll board with Obatola as soon as she's packed and ready. "

A resounding *no* screamed in his head. There had to be another solution. If it had been anyone else, would he be struggling with the decision taken by men who would have him court-martialled if he didn't do their bidding?

Was he ready to give up his career to keep her off the ship? The navy was where he'd found purpose and meaning. Once he'd joined, he'd never looked back or thought about doing anything else. Until now.

All because he wanted to keep the woman he'd just met and thought he'd never see again out of harm's way. He didn't appreciate Dubem's silence about the situation.

Akin felt the need to at least try to circumvent the decision.

"It's unorthodox." More like crazy as hell and possibly the worst idea anyone had ever come up with. "The risk to her if we're attacked is too great."

He wouldn't bring up the inherent risks she could face from the men on board. Sailors weren't known for being kind or gentle, especially when on tour. It took one of their kind to deal with them. Although she'd appeared strong, he'd sensed a fracture within her. She wouldn't be able to handle the men.

"Isn't there another way?"

Captain stared until Akin yielded his gaze and looked down at the desk.

"Can you think of a solution which would allow us to continue with our work of pursuing some of the most dangerous and daring pirates on the sea?"

The question didn't need an answer. "We could head out without involving an innocent civilian. We still have a nurse and medic on board."

At the captain's nod, Dubem tapped on his tablet. "Former reservist Comfort Djan from the British Royal Army joined the ranks of the Royal Army Medical Corp as a Second Lieutenant after completing officer training and graduating medical school."

"She's no more a civilian than either you or I." Captain pointed an index finger in Akin's direction. "I don't doubt she would've one day outranked you if she'd gone in full time as had been her intention before tragedy stuck. Her records are exemplary, and she had nothing but high commendations."

Once again impressed with the woman he'd been instantly attracted to, his ears perked up at the word tragedy. What had happened to her?

"How can we place her in danger?"

"She does it by choice by working with MSF. The woman dives head first into areas devastated by war and ravaged by disease. She volunteered to come to The Gambia during an Ebola virus outbreak. It doesn't sound as if she fears anything. Since there's been no new cases in about a month, her superior at MSF has granted her a special dispensation for her to work with us."

Akin's jaw ached from the clenching. There was nothing he could do to keep her out of danger. They'd already made up their minds, so what was he doing in this meeting?

"She's a soldier through and through. A woman of duty who after being briefed, understands the importance of this mission." Captain Obot stood and used his position in an attempt to intimidate. "I'm holding you responsible for her safety, Commander."

Rather than be cowed, Akin claimed his unwanted assignment. "Yes, sir."

On my honour, I'll protect her with my life.

He was stuck in the political machinations of men who wanted to ensure they got their money's worth from their multi-million-dollar naval investment.

With anger boiling his blood to where he felt feverish and neared the point of losing his hard-earned discipline, he stood. He took his leave without asking the fifty other questions torpedoing through his mind.

Do without complaint.

CHAPTER FIVE

In an attempt to maintain her composure, Comfort smoothed down her hair as she tore her gaze away from the massive ship. Or at least tried to. More ship met her vision as they approached it from the dinghy.

What had she expected? Not the grey monstrosity that faced her.

Granted, it didn't extend to the mammoth size of the battleship she'd toured in the UK years ago. She'd been told that this destroyer, known as *Reckoning*, was used for its speed and fighting manoeuvrability. Its size gave her pause to believe that they'd chosen the correct ship for their task.

They'd reached the side of the vessel. Once on board, she focused her attention on the job she'd signed up for and followed as two men flanked Ishaq, helping him to walk. The going was slow, but he insisted on being on his own two feet rather than carried on a stretcher.

The wind whipped around her as the hair at the back of her neck stood on end. The man she'd hoped to avoid when she'd taken the job stood before her.

Or had she agreed to the crazy stint because of him?

No. She'd decided to take the position because of the adventure it presented. Something different which might help sweep away the unfailing gloom. A chance to work with the armed forces once again. She'd missed the strict discipline of the institution. The camaraderie and belonging of being a soldier.

It had all been snatched away from her. She cleared her head with a deep inhale of sea air.

"Welcome aboard, Dr. Djan."

The deep huskiness of his voice sent a trickle of heat down her spine. "Thank you, Commander Solarin."

He glared down at her. Had she upset him by mispronouncing his name?

"Although you have the qualifications, you're not considered military while on board this ship. You may call me Akin. This extends to all personnel aboard except Captain Obot."

"Noted. Then everyone can call me Comfort."

His light eyes sparkled as the corners of his lips twitched up for a flash, as if entertained, before his expression returned to stern. "Doctor. We'll call you any derivative of that. The men need to keep in mind who you are and your mission with us."

She arched a brow. "And the women?"

The jerk of his head revealed genuine surprise.

"This is a vessel designated for apprehending pirates. There are no women on the ship." The muscle in his jaw jumped. "Until now."

The grumble of those last words indicated he wasn't happy to have her on board.

Not a problem. She'd stay out of his way.

She placed a hand against her upper arm and snuck in a pinch. Was she really on a multi-government sanctioned ship intended to fight pirates? For the first time in years, a true sense of excitement hovered in her chest.

She held herself stiff, as if at full attention, when she glanced around to find herself the object of blatant stares. About twenty crew members surrounded them. Some of them smiled when she met their gazes. The frowns on a good number of faces told her Akin wasn't the only one who was unhappy with her being on board. She couldn't miss the lascivious looks of more than a few as they raked their gaze over her body. If they thought she'd provide them with anything more than her medical expertise, they'd learn a blistering lesson.

Standing within Akin's shadow, she had no fear about being the sole female. As the only fully functional medical doctor, she doubted any of the men were idiotic enough to risk losing her. She was no fool to think everyone would like her, but the nature of military was to protect. The majority would most likely be as protective as her twin brothers had been.

She swallowed down the ache the intrusive thought induced. Pushing away the pain thinking about her family always brought, she attempted to pay closer attention to her surroundings as they walked along the ship.

They descended a steep metal staircase which she had no shame going down backwards. Her resemblance to a toddler as she took her time, clinging to the rails, made her smile. At the bottom, they tucked around a left, then a right turn before standing in front of an open door where she peeped a hospital bed. A man nearly as tall as Akin, but not as broad-shouldered, stepped up to them. She couldn't help thinking she'd have to get accustomed to feeling dwarfed while on the ship.

"This is our nurse, Midshipman Ancille Barre," Akin introduced. "Meet Dr. Djan."

Interesting how he'd left out her first name. Ancille seemed lost as to how to greet her.

She dipped her head in his direction. As a healthcare worker, he should understand about shaking hands with a stranger during this time of Ebola. "It's nice to meet you."

He returned the head dip. "You, too, Dr. Djan."

"Show her around the medical station," Akin ordered. "I'll be back for her in fifteen minutes."

Without a look in Comfort's direction, he rotated and strode in the opposite direction they'd come.

Understanding the weight of leadership, she didn't question his coldness. It still didn't stop his actions from stinging. She'd met him yesterday. Why would anything he did matter to her? It shouldn't, and from this point out, she'd ensure it didn't.

Ancille led the way into the rather large medical room. She held in a whistle as her attention drifted to the technology which rivalled any she'd worked with in the hospitals in Britain. Two high-tech hospital beds stood locked on one side of the room. On the other side sat a desk with a computer on it. A small area beyond the beds held a collapsible stretcher, a tiny table, and two chairs for what she'd consider a claustrophobic consulting room. Their equipment was most likely stored in strategically placed cabinets.

Ishaq had been settled into the bed farthest from the door and appeared to be sleeping. The journey had to have zapped his energy. In ideal conditions, he would've been lying in bed with intermittent short walks, not a trip on the ocean. Ancille gave her the recording of Ishaq's vital signs without her having to ask.

"I checked his dressing and marked the drainage. I'll keep an eye on it. He claimed to have no pain." Ancille shook his head. "Doc's as stoic as they come. He's resting without cussing up a storm, so the pain must be manageable."

Smiling, Comfort predicted that she'd enjoy working with Ancille. There was nothing she liked more than efficiency. "I had them change the dressing this morning and them remove the drain. The exertion of coming onto the ship must've caused seepage. We'll just have to ensure that he splints it when he does his breathing and coughing exercises." She turned to Ishaq. "Is that clear, Doctor?"

He put his hand on the small pillow they'd placed on his abdomen and took in a deep breath, wincing as he coughed to prevent postsurgical pneumonia. "Yes, Doctor Djan. I'm sure you'll be a pain in the ass about it, so I may as well just get it done."

She laughed as she returned her attention to Ancille.

The nurse spoke with pride as he took her on a tour of her new work environment ending with their full supply closet. "We even have a morgue, but it only fits three."

She blinked up at him in shock before collecting her composure. Now, she'd know to expect anything on this ship. She rubbed her bare arms. "It's so cold in here."

Ancille nodded.

"The whole ship is air-conditioned. Otherwise, the atmosphere would be stale and sweltering." He plucked at the sleeve of his uniform. "It's not so bad when we wear these."

Looking down at her orange, short-sleeved cotton blouse and black linen slacks, it was a wonder her teeth weren't clanging together with shivers. She'd been working in warm climates for a couple of years. Other than her white lab coat, she didn't own anything which would keep goose bumps from making a constant presence on her skin.

Her eyes widened. "What about the sleeping quarters?"

"Same. They gave us standard issue sheets, pillows, and blankets, so sleeping is comfortable. At least, as good as it's going to get while sharing a room with twelve other people." His head shake indicated it wasn't his favourite aspect about being in the navy. "I'm sure they'll set you up with what you need."

Comfort let out a breath. Nights were tough enough without having to worry about suffering from hypothermia.

At least, she'd escaped the monotony of the hospital outpatient routine of the past few weeks and found a bit of adventure to stave off the restlessness. It would help take her mind off the grief which weighed heavy on her when she wasn't sufficiently occupied. She could sense the good of what was to come.

As long as she stayed away from hostile sailors and downplayed the attraction lingering between her and Akin, the time she'd agreed to work for the West African Sea Protection Alliance would be manageable. Yet, even at that moment, she wanted him to be hovering near her. For his intense gaze to warm her to her toes.

Maintaining distance between them would save her in the end. With his career as a navy officer, he didn't seem the sort of man who would commit, and she wasn't the kind of woman who'd survive another loss. A chill, which had nothing to do with the cold air, snaked down her spine. The familiar press of guilt that lingered and darkened every moment of her life never allowed her to forget that she'd been the one to survive a tragedy which should've killed her, while others had not.

CHAPTER SIX

Akin wished he could send Comfort back to the safety of The Gambia. Not that a country which had been ravaged by Ebola could be considered safe. Yet, it was better than having her at sea. Putting her at risk for encountering unscrupulous pirates. Even worse, the appetites of men who lived without women for much too long at a stretch.

No one would dare attack her. Not while she was under his protection. The one thing he couldn't control was her choosing someone other than him to be with. He'd relegated her to being someone to guard, not as a potential lover. The fact that the only woman he'd been attracted to in a very long time would be in close proximity didn't diminish his dread at having her on board.

Why was he the only one to see that it was a bad idea all around? Not even the good doctor had had the sense to decline the position when offered. Who in their right mind would accept such a job?

I did.

He ignored the words his mind threw at him. Having been in the navy since eighteen, he'd been prepared for this post. As a reservist in the army and then having left, she wasn't.

The promise he'd made to the captain held firm—he'd keep her safe. No matter what.

Annoyed at the situation she'd gotten herself into, he breezed into the sick bay. He stopped short at the sight of Comfort's full lips widened into a smile as she listened to Ancille. His chest tightened, and the need to lift her into his arms and swim with her back to shore brought a haze to his vision. She didn't belong where danger loomed every second of the day.

He'd do his damnedest to ensure she made it through this mission unharmed.

Being the first to notice him, Ancille stood at attention.

"At ease," he ordered while maintaining his sights on the doctor. "Come with me."

As if in slow motion, all traces of the smile she'd just worn disappeared. A stern mask took its place. Arms rose and crossed under her chest, lifting perfect breasts upward. His attention dove to the mango-sized orbs, wondering if they'd taste as sweet as the fruit they resembled. He flung his gaze back to her eyes.

A storm brewed in them as she took up a wide-legged stance.

Ancille must've sensed the trouble about to erupt because he shuffled towards the only patient in the room.

Her stare-down heated his skin. What was the problem?

"Let's go. I'm going to show you around the ship."

Turning to the exit, he expected her to follow. He'd made it three meters down the hallway when he realized she hadn't joined him.

His temper spiked. Other than the captain and the other commanders, everyone on the ship followed his orders. Without question. As a civilian who had once served in the army reserves, he expected the same from her. It was the only way he could ensure her safety. He had to consider her as part of the crew, not a female he wanted to draw against him and kiss the deep frown from, teasing until she moulded her luscious curves against him and opened her mouth to allow him to taste her heat and passion.

As he shook his head, the impossible thought disappeared as he re-entered the sick bay. The scene remained the same. Ancille stood by Ishaq's bed, and the princess remained planted.

Three strides carried him from the door to within half an arm's length of her. Utilizing his towering height as a show of power, he put on his most menacing glower. Men's voices had quivered when he'd looked at them in such a manner. The doctor glared up at him with her own squinted stare.

He shouldn't notice how her eyes weren't as dark as he'd initially thought. Or how her scent reminded him of a flower in full bloom, attracting bees and butterflies with its fragrance. Or how he wanted to end the stalemate by lowering his head and closing the space between their lips. Would they be as soft as he'd imagined? Yielding under his?

"Commander Solarin."

The call barely pierced his concentration. He turned his attention from the woman who enticed him with her obstinate nature. How many females were strong enough to stand up to him? Hell, there were men who couldn't claim the honour.

He flung his attention to the man he considered to be closer than a brother. "What!"

Ancille's shoulder's jerked back. The movement returned Akin's equilibrium.

Ishaq's lips had a slight upward tilt to them. Was the bastard laughing?

"Due to my unfortunate incapacitation, Dr. Djan has been brought on ship as a civilian. She holds rank as a professional just as you do as a naval officer."

Comfort's nod in his periphery irritated him.

Ishaq raised his hand and cleared his throat. The corners of his eyes crinkled in what could only be humour. Once the man was cleared to physically train again, Akin would make him pay.

"Dr. Djan. We truly appreciate your presence with us. As a former army reservist, you're aware of the hierarchy and structure of the military. Kindly excuse us for overlooking your civilian presence in our midst. Orders are all we know. They keep us safe when others want to do us harm. It's nothing personal."

Miraculously, her arms fell to her sides, her shoulders relaxed, and the stony expression melted. "Thank you for the reminder."

They'd both been duly chastised without the destruction of their egos. Something Ishaq excelled at. He wasn't known as the heart of the ship for nothing. Almost everyone loved him.

Now to move forward with the mutinous doctor.

"I'll show you around the ship and to your cabin so you can settle in. And then, we'll eat lunch. The captain has scheduled a meeting with you and the other commanders at fourteen hundred hours." Did she understand military time? "That's two o'clock."

Her nostrils flared, and he thought they'd have another standoff. The thought of a potential confrontation set off a spark of excitement in his belly.

"I'm aware of military time, thank you."

Her voice came out calm and cultured, just as it had when they'd sat in her office yesterday. Had it been less than twenty-four hours since they'd met?

"I'm looking forward to taking a tour of the ship. It's a lot bigger than I imagined," she continued.

Proud of the vessel he served on, Akin pulled his shoulders back. "*Reckoning* is one of the most modern ships this side of the Atlantic."

"I see. This infirmary is state of the art and well stocked. I can already tell it won't be a burden working here." She turned to Ancille "I'll be back after my meeting with the captain. I've left the treatment orders. Please contact me if you need me."

Then, she turned to Akin with her brows furrowed. "How will he get in contact with me?"

He held back a chuckle at her expression. Confusion looked adorable on her. Not as attractive as when she smiled, but much better than when she dug her heels in to get her way. He pointed to a phone hanging on the wall. "Each room has a phone. We'll either call or pipe you."

"What?"

Chuckles came from Ancille and Ishaq as Akin ducked his head to hide his amusement.

Ishaq winced as he placed a hand over a pillow on his abdomen. "Make an announcement through the ship's speakers."

Comfort looked up at Akin. "You guys have your own language."

"Yes, we do. You're intelligent. I'm sure it won't take long to grasp."

She blinked at him as if surprised and then nodded. "Okay. I'm ready to go when you are."

His head tingled at the words. If only things were different.

What would he do? Charm her. Ha. He didn't have the skill, but he could get her to like him... with time. The farfetched possibility had been snatched from him. His job consisted of guarding and protecting, not seducing. He'd do well to maintain a constant stream of reminders towards his body.

Akin turned and walked out the door. This time, her light, alluring scent indicated that she'd followed.

CHAPTER SEVEN

Comfort had difficulty closing her mouth after being dragged all over the ship. From the kitchen to the bridge, she'd been impressed by every facet of her temporary home. The questions brewed. It would've made sense to ask her enforced tour guide what she wanted to know, but she'd thought better of it.

After their altercation in the sick bay, she'd concluded that it was mandatory that they stay on opposite sides of the ship. His domineering presence made her uncomfortable, yet, she felt safe with him. Formidable in her own right when her temper became riled, she could see fights breaking out between them if they spent too much time together. She didn't need anyone upsetting the miniscule amount of peace she'd striven to obtain.

Akin opened the door to one of many rooms down a passageway. "This is your cabin."

She stepped into the space and looked around. Not what she'd expected. Her luggage had been placed in a corner. A desk, wardrobe, and single elevated bed attached to the wall filled the rest of the small space. Chest constricted, she had trouble breathing. Her hands shook as a trickle of panic moistened her palms.

"I'll be alone." Hating the quiver in her voice, she avoided looking into his face.

He moved to stand in front of her. "What's wrong?"

The tenderness in his tone made her raise her head in order to ensure he'd been the one who'd spoken. His eyes spoke of a kindness he hadn't shown before. A responding softness stirred in her.

How could she explain her terror without sounding weak? From what she knew about him, he wouldn't appreciate it. "I thought I'd be with other people. In bunks."

A crease formed in his forehead as his brows drew close. "There are crew members who would throw someone off the ship to get their own cabin."

Sleeping alone wasn't an option. Insomnia ruled her nights. When she did sleep, the nightmares woke her, and she needed the knowledge that someone was around in order for her to calm down. Otherwise, panic overtook her, making her physically ill. The person never had to wake up in order to bring her comfort; their presence alone did the job.

"I'd prefer to sleep where others are."

He cocked his head and studied her. "You're the only female on board this ship. There's no way in hell I'll let you sleep anywhere but by yourself."

Ire rose. Comfort braced her hands on her hips. "I thought it was your job, Commander, to keep me happy and comfortable while I'm saving your asses. I need to be around people."

Why hadn't she asked how many women would be on the ship? In a rush to escape monotony, memories, and guilt, she'd jumped into her new adventure without getting the details.

His Adam's apple bobbed. What words had he swallowed? She'd never know.

His "Why?" came out rough and harassed.

She let her hands slip down her sides as the tightness in her shoulders loosened. He was trying to not engage in a fight—she may as well do the same. It would make her stay on the vessel a lot more enjoyable.

"I'm not a fan of sleeping alone when I'm in strange places." *Or anytime.* "I haven't done it in years. Not since I joined *Médecins Sans Frontières*." Before that, she'd lived with her now ex-husband until he'd decided to leave her because he couldn't handle the unrecoverable mess she'd turned into. "I always opt to have a roommate."

His features relaxed as if he'd accepted the partial truth. "Isn't being alone a luxury?"

"Maybe if I wasn't in a steel cage."

She tried another tact and rested her hand on his arm ... then snatched it back at the electric current that raced into her. Her heart sped, and she wanted to experience the thrilling sensation again. It wouldn't happen because he'd backed up, leaving the distance of the room between them.

"Is there anything you could do so I don't have to sleep alone? Maybe I could sleep on the bridge." At least, someone would always be around even if she woke up sore from lying on the floor.

His lips pursed. "You do remember what the bridge is, right?"

Not caring for his sarcastic tone, she snarled. "Of course I do. Now you can see that I'm serious about not sleeping alone. I just can't," she ended softly.

What did his loud sigh signify? What were her options if he didn't change the sleeping arrangements?

The tension in the room grew thick as the silence stretched. Would she have to ask the captain to let her off the ship? They'd already set sail. Returning her would leave them without a doctor on board.

His deep voice startled her. "Have you always been afraid to sleep alone?"

"No."

"Does it have anything to do with the tragedy you went through?" As if realizing he'd stepped over a line he had no right to cross, he waved a hand. "Never mind. That's none of my business."

Better that he made the admission than she having to tell him off for it. One thing she didn't miss about the military was their ability to discover everything about a person's life. Privacy didn't exist. Agreeing to join this ship, even for a short time, had ensconced her back into that lifestyle. At least, he seemed to know that something had happened to her family.

Maybe she should try to sleep by herself.

Comfort clenched cold fingers against her stomach as it rolled with dread. She hated the debilitating fear more than anything. Yet, she found herself powerless when it came to defeating it. No. She wasn't ready to sleep alone. Would she ever be? A year of therapy had helped, but not to the point where she considered herself normal again. Would it ever happen?

Akin wiped a hand down his face. "How do you feel about small spaces?"

She released the breath she'd been holding. "I don't have a problem with them."

A grunt was his only response.

Claustrophobia wasn't an issue while the fear of waking up alone terrified her.

"Okay. I'll have to speak with Lewis." He must've read the confusion on her face because he clarified. "He runs Logistics. He'd be your boss if you were navy. You'll meet him along with Gowon this afternoon. The new accommodations will be arranged by the time the meeting is over. For now, let's go to lunch."

Relieved, she smiled as they headed out the door. "Where will I be sleeping?"

He angled his wide shoulders to look at her. "With me."

CHAPTER EIGHT

Why would a mature, travelled woman be afraid to sleep by herself?

The question never left Akin as he escorted Comfort to the cafeteria for lunch. Her face didn't scream her age, but with the limited information the captain had given him, he'd calculated her to be in her early thirties. She hadn't explained why she needed someone in the room with her. His imagination went wild. Maybe she'd been attacked while sleeping. Or she had a phobia which she couldn't overcome.

No speculation sat right. She was too strong of a woman to allow fear to overwhelm her. Then again, what did he know about her other than she possessed the reputation of being a great doctor and stubborn as hell? Beautiful to the point of distraction, with dark, penetrating eyes tinged with pain that invited him to fall into them.

He'd given up his cabin for her, and yet, the turn of events was a bigger inconvenience. They'd have to share the same sleeping quarters. He didn't trust anyone else to do it. His promise to protect her held him bound. After his talk with Lewis via radio, some of the crew had been shifted from the four-man berthing cabin so he and Comfort could share the space.

"The meal was delicious." Comfort's appreciation broke into his thoughts. "I didn't expect the food to be so good."

Akin took in their empty plates. He'd eaten on autopilot. "Food is a big part of keeping morale up while we're at sea."

"Someone should inform the army because that's not how they roll."

His laughter escaped, sounding a bit rusty even to his own ears. The woman had a way of entertaining him.

Sobering quickly, he pointed to her plate. "Will you go for more?"

Her eyes widened. "We can have seconds?"

The attempt to hold back a smile failed, and he let it linger.

"As much as you want. Hungry sailors do shoddy work. It's all about making sure they're happy so the work gets done efficiently." Glancing around the room, he observed the men talking and laughing. All of them were stealing glances in Comfort's direction. "We don't get much in the way of pleasure around here, so we do what we can to limit the men's homesickness and dips in mood."

"Makes sense. Since they can't be around their family, friends, or significant others, they may as well eat to their heart's content."

He recognized the sadness in her eyes which had never left. What had happened to her? How could he make things better? The question startled him into standing and grabbing his tray.

"Let's get going."

She mimicked him as they took care of their food scraps, plates, utensils, and tray.

Why did it matter how she felt? He'd met her yesterday, and now, they worked together. Sure, he'd liked her from the first moment he'd relaxed enough to assess her in the Emergency Room. The moment he'd known Ishaq had proper care. She'd been calm and competent as she'd treated him. Plus, she hadn't been intimidated by him. Such a woman deserved respect.

She walked at his side as they headed towards the conference room. "I could've done without being stared at while we ate."

"A beautiful woman on a ship full of male sailors has got to expect some stares."

As long as they didn't do anything more, they wouldn't encounter any repercussions from him.

Her hand flew to the scar on her forehead as she dipped her head. "It's disconcerting."

At least, she didn't deny her looks. Even with the marred skin, she was a stunner.

"The only way I could get them to stop looking at you is to gouge their eyes out." He halted and pinned her with a mock menacing stare. "Is that what you want?"

She quirked her lips to the side as she considered it. Then, she let out a giggle which sounded too girlish to have come from her very womanly mouth. "As much as I'd prefer if they didn't stare, I wouldn't want to give you the extra job, which I would then have to take care of. So thanks, but no."

He maintained his false stern expression, wishing the exchange could continue. When was the last time he'd enjoyed bantering with a woman?

On a serious note, he said, "As honourable as I'd like to think the men are, I can't vouch for all of them. If you have any complaints about a single one of them, tell me."

She nodded, but he didn't believe her. She seemed the type of person to keep her own confidences and take care of her own problems. He didn't doubt that she could, either, but he'd prefer to do it for her. Solely because it was his duty, nothing more.

The next point, he needed to ensure that she adhere to. He looked her straight in the eyes. "Can you promise me that you won't walk the ship alone? If I'm not around, then I'll make sure someone I trust is."

"Since you asked so nicely, even though you could've stepped it up a notch with a please. I agree to having an escort and not walk the boat—"

"—ship."

"— alone." Her eyes sparkled. "Although I don't like the fact that I'll always have a bodyguard hovering over me. What if I want some privacy?"

"Aren't you the one who wants to share a cabin instead of being in your own?"

Opening her mouth as if to speak, she closed it and strode in the direction they'd been headed. "We should get to the meeting."

What had he said to shut down the camaraderie they'd shared only a minute ago? His curiosity raged. He'd find out the reason. Even if it took him saying a blasted please for her to open up.

Comfort sat at the rectangular conference table with Akin to her left. He'd introduced her to Commander Cheikou Gowon, in charge of marine engineering when they'd walked in. The man had briefly lifted his nose from his tablet to say hello before ignoring them as they waited for the others to arrive.

Things had been going well between her and Akin. And then, he'd had to mention her fear of sleeping alone. Not something that brought pride into her heart. If she could've gotten over it, she would've. But the ghosts of the past refused to stop haunting her.

Or am I the one hanging onto them?

A man strode in. Since no one stood, she presumed he wasn't the captain. Akin made the introductions to Commander Deyma Lewis who nodded when he sat. Her scalp prickled as his cold eyes studied her face and then seemed to dismiss her as insignificant.

"Welcome on board, Dr. Djan," he said in a grim voice which clearly placed him in the category of one of the soldiers who resented her presence.

The testosterone in the room might crush her. It didn't help that all three men, in their varying ways, were handsome. The freckles across Gowon's nose where his glasses sat took him to a level of adorable she didn't want to analyse. Like the others, Lewis wore no facial hair, but his strong jawline added to his ruggedness.

She ignored both her reaction and his tone. "Please call me Comfort."

"We'll all call you Doctor."

Akin repeated the same thing he'd insisted on when she'd stepped onto the ship. Was his voice gruffer than normal?

Lewis' teeth sparkled with his too wide smile as if overcompensating for his initial behaviour. "Thank you for deciding to come on board. We couldn't undertake this return mission without you."

"When duty calls, you must answer," she responded.

"Sounds like a true military personnel." He leaned his upper body across the table. "I recommend you return to the fold. This time, join the navy. It's a better service. I'm sure you'd be a great asset to the men."

She schooled her features to hide her surprise at the term men versus service. What had he meant by that last part? There was something dark in his eyes that made her straighten her back, ready to fight. Although he'd done nothing wrong, she neither liked nor trusted him. That told her enough, considering she got along with most people. She'd found in the past that the people she didn't like upon their first meeting had a reason not to be trusted. Staying away from him while on board would be best. Looked like she'd be spending her time running away from people. At least, the ship was big enough.

"I'll think about it."

"Good to hear. I've changed your accommodations. You and Commander Solarin will be bunking together in a four-man Mess. The men have cleared out. I can't give you your own head or shower, but I'll ensure that whenever you'd like to shower, you will be alone. Are you okay with that?"

Maybe it was the high-pitched tone of his voice that made it feel as if ants were playing on her skin. She didn't care for the way he'd smirked when he'd mentioned her and Akin bunking together. It wasn't as if anything would happen between them. Akin had already displayed that he didn't like her, and she found his perpetual glaring to be annoying. Her psyche downplayed the part about his smile making her insides go warm and those electric shocks when they'd touched. Those had to be isolated incidences which wouldn't be repeated. Besides, with their jobs taking up so many hours in the day, they'd only be together when sleeping.

"Yes. I'm sure it will be fine," she answered. If they didn't kill each other, leaving the ship without a doctor and a commander of... what did he do?

"Thank you for making the arrangements." Not willing to speak to Lewis again, she turned to Akin. "What are you a commander of?"

Gowon snorted. "Kicking our asses."

The dig from the man she thought had been lost to whatever resided on his tablet deepened Akin's frown.

"Warfare."

She nodded as a light of understanding shone. "Of course."

It explained his protectiveness and coarse personality. The man had to be stern in order to ensure the survival of the men in battle.

All of a sudden, the three men stood as if pulled by puppet strings. She turned to the door and did the same, stopping her arm midway in a salute. Old habits were sometimes harder to break than one would think.

Comfort's eyes widened when Dubem tailed the captain into the room and stood at his right-hand side.

Their leader sat and indicated with a wave of the hand that they should, too. "Welcome on board, Dr. Djan. I'm Captain Emmanuel Obot. We appreciate you coming to our assistance with your medical expertise and combat skills. Hopefully, we'll only utilize the more peaceful aspect while you're on the ship."

The most powerful man on the ship didn't reach the others in height, but he no less resonated power from his lean body. Grey hair mixed their way over his short crew cut, and light lines grooved into his face, giving away his age as being somewhere in his early fifties, if not later. He wouldn't be one to cross without severe consequences.

"Thank you, Captain. I'll take good care of your men."

Lewis snorted, acquiring a narrow-eyed glare from the captain while the rest ignored him as if it were his normal behaviour. Maybe he was the one with the psychological problems rather than Dubem.

Captain Obot returned his attention to her.

"That's what I like to hear. We're hoping you won't be treating anything more major than their general aches and pains from hard work." He slid a manila envelope across the table. "Here's your contract. Please read it and give it back to me by the end of the day."

Not giving her a chance to reply, he continued. "I take it you've been introduced to the other commanders and escorted on a tour of the ship."

"Yes, sir."

"Please let me know through one of my commanders if you need anything. How are your accommodations?"

Instinct told her that he didn't actually care and had more pressing issues to attend to, so she nodded. "Everything is fine, sir. I'm sure I'll be comfortable while aboard your ship."

"Good. Solarin will escort you to the sick bay and then return."

After the crisp dismissal, she picked up the envelope from the table and stood. She patted her hair to make sure it was still in place after the whirlwind personality she'd just encountered.

"I should've warned you," Akin said as they walked down the corridor.

No, she corrected herself, the passageway. The walls with all sorts of equipment crowded against them were referred to as bulkheads, while the stairs were ladders. She'd continue to call them stairs.

She looked up at him. "It would've been nice to have a heads up that your captain is a tornado, cyclone, and a hurricane combined."

His chuckle surprised her, and the warmth she'd tried to play off just moments ago as an anomaly rippled through her body and settled low in her belly. His persona changed when he laughed. She shouldn't like it, but she couldn't help wanting to make him happy.

He increased their pace. "He's excellent at his job."

She heard the respect in his voice and instinctively knew Captain Obot was one of the few he trusted. "What does Dubem do on the ship?"

"He's the Executive Officer."

She tripped over one of the many hatch doors littering the passageway. He grabbed her just in time to stop her from ripping down the equipment lining the walls. He'd had to pull her against his firm body, and she liked being there way too much. Rather than lean into him like she wanted, she peeled herself away and stepped to the side.

He cleared his throat and put even more space between them as they walked. "Dubem may seem carefree, light-hearted, and at times, too honest for his own good, but he's one of the hardest workers and best leaders this ship could ever have. I consider him to be a good friend."

At the sick bay, the corners of Akin's mouth had taken up their pursed position, and his eyes had hardened. "If you need to leave, call me. Ancille knows where I'll be. I'll either come or send someone. You will always have someone in the sick bay working with you. I trust them all to ensure your safety."

Why the hell did she feel like a child being taught about stranger danger? Rather than release the sarcastic *Yes, sir* which wanted to fly off her tongue, she nodded and entered her new work space.

Things would be fine between them if Akin could maintain his curt, over-protective demeanour at all times. Things started to break down during the rare occasions when he acted like a normal person with an actual heart and sense of humour. She didn't want to see him as more than a naval officer she had to work with.

Not that she'd ever get involved with him, or anyone else on the ship. The pain of loss of loved ones ripping her apart in the past wouldn't allow it. Everyone she'd ever loved had left her, leaving her feeling guilty and utterly alone. She'd never allow it to happen again.

CHAPTER NINE

An hour after Akin's departure, Comfort had come to the conclusion that working as a medic on the ship would be a lot more fascinating than a hospital outpatient department. Ancille and Ishaq had given her a thorough orientation on how the ship's sick bay ran and what her duties included.

"Ishaq, would you feel more comfortable in your cabin?" She'd learned that as the ship's doctor, he had his own accommodation, like the commanders and captain. "One of us could check on you every few hours."

He placed a hand to his mouth to cover a yawn. "Are you discharging me?"

"With all the activity of today, no. You need the rest, and I don't want you overexerting yourself and making me replace those sutures. I figured you'd feel more at home in your cabin."

The gruff laugh was followed by a groan as he held his abdomen. "You don't know these men yet, but you will. If I went to my room, they'd feel obligated to visit me, aka disturb me. I'll get more rest here. And—" he winked, "—the mattress is more comfortable, and I don't have to do a thing to prop myself up. It happens with the press of a button."

Comfort chuckled. She welcomed his company. Not just because of his friendliness, but he could guide her in the job for the first couple of days. "As you wish, Dr. Obatola."

He clutched his heart and moaned with the flair of a stage actor. "Now I'm beginning to think you want to drive me out of here by using my last name."

"Just showing respect."

"Ha." He hitched a thumb towards the door. "I get enough of that from them. I'd like a friend for the short time you're on board."

How long had it been since she'd made a true friend? Yes, the man would be wonderful to hang around. "How long do you think it will take us to get to Lagos?'

His expression became sombre as he shrugged.

"I don't know. It depends on what we meet on the way back, or the assignment we're given. I don't think the captain is any kind of rush." He shrugged again. "Maybe a week."

She'd hoped it would be for a little longer. She liked the environment, and so far, most of the men she'd encountered had been nice. Akin only partially fit in that category because he set her on edge.

"How long are you usually out to sea?"

"It depends on the tour and what we encounter," Ancille said. "I think the longest we've been out was six weeks. It was one of the first tours we'd done. We did a lot of apprehensions and captures. The pirates take us more seriously now, so they've become more ingenious with their attempts."

A sailor stepped into the room, and she attended to him.

When the patient left and she finished the computer work, she turned to find Ishaq's gaze fixated on her.

"I have a feeling that for the next few days, the sick bay is going to be busy."

"Why?" she asked.

"Some of these men will have legitimate complaints, but they'll be coming to take a look at you. Maybe see if they have a chance at catching and claiming your attention outside of the sick bay." He shifted in the bed with a grunt. "Should be entertaining."

Ignoring the heat creeping up her neck to her face as easily as she did Ishaq, she attended to another patient who'd come in while Ancille dealt with another. When the sailor that Ancille was about to tend to suddenly stated that he had work to complete and would be back later, she avoided looking in Ishaq's chuckling direction.

As the men trickled in over the next few hours, she put her foot down and refused to let any of them go without being assessed. They would either be seen by Ancille or not at all.

The majority of men were starved for attention. No one could claim her to be the most compassionate person in the world, but she knew how to smile, share a joke, and most of all, listen.

She'd had to put the three who'd openly flirted with her in their place by telling them in no uncertain terms that she could only be their doctor or friend and nothing more. She was glad for Ishaq's growl of support. Two had taken it well.

The last, Acting Sub-Lieutenant Umale—the most handsome and youngest of the three—had made her skin crawl when he'd sat and stroked her hand as if he'd had the right. She'd wanted to stab her pen into the back of his hand. In his mid-twenties, he'd stared at her breasts as he'd leaned closer and spoken low enough for only her to hear.

"I'm not into old women, but I'd like to give you a chance at the hottest sex that will ever come your way. We'll *talk* later."

Before she could get over the shock of his words and blast him with her own, he'd sauntered out of the room. His audacity had made her feel like scrubbing her skin until she felt clean.

She rubbed her hands along her arms, the goose bumps due more to the despicable man than the cool air. She never wanted to experience the insecurities his treatment had elicited again. If she could help it, she wouldn't.

Brushing off the man's actions as loneliness-induced, she continued with her paperwork. If he tried such a stunt again, she'd know how to handle it. With the use of debilitating pressure points. She'd make sure to start with words. Always begin with words.

At seven, one last soldier came in. Ancille introduced him as the medic, Chief Hospital Corpsman Gideon Asiedu.

Recognizing a fellow Ghanaian, she asked him how he was doing in Twi, the most commonly spoken language in Ghana. "*Wo ho te sɛn?*"

An instant smile appeared, showing off straight teeth and brightening his round face. "*Me ho ye. Na wo nso ɛ?*"

"Ɛyɛ." She'd told him she was fine after his response of him being well followed with a question of how she was doing.

Just as she was about to say more in their local language, all the fun got sucked out of the room with the presence of Akin's bulky body filling the doorway.

"Asiedu, you know the rules about speaking indigenous languages on board this ship."

Gideon stood at spine-cracking attention. "Yes, sir."

"I started it." She defended her parents' countryman. For once, thinking about her parents didn't make her feel as if a hot spear had gone through her heart. She'd used what they'd taught her over the years while living in Brighton in an attempt to maintain their language, and she felt proud.

Akin didn't look in her direction. "He should've ended it. He's aware of how it causes division and cliques when unity is of the utmost importance to achieve our aim."

"Yes, sir."

"At ease."

She bit the inside of her cheek to hold in her protest. How could he irritate her so easily? She'd never been as reactive to anyone. Not even her siblings had been able to rile her in such a manner, and they'd known exactly which buttons to push. This man did it without knowing a thing about her. Unfair treatment of others stood among the top of her pet peeves.

She whirled away from Akin and went to Gideon. "I'm here to serve the crew. Please don't hesitate to contact me when necessary."

The friendliness he'd shown previously had vanished. "Yes, Doctor."

She held her tongue. Why could she call them by their first names and not have it reciprocated? The brute she'd now call a cabin mate had made the decree, and they would follow it. Instead of cutting her eyes at Akin or engaging in some other disrespectful act, she went to Ishaq.

"He's an excellent soldier, but an even better man. One of the most loyal and dedicated people you could ever be privileged to call a friend," Ishaq said in lowered voice for her ears alone. "Just a bit...rough."

Hadn't Dubem said the exact same thing? "Huh. It's possible only one of us will make it out of the cabin tomorrow. I'm putting my money on me."

The doctor's light chuckle calmed her and drew the attention of the other men. "It is well."

She blinked and swallowed hard at hearing her mother's favourite saying. "Yes, it is. Make sure to take your pain meds and antibiotics when Gideon gives them to you. I need you up and about as soon as possible."

His gaze held hers. "You did well today. You seemed to innately know what the men needed. Our role is both physician and counsellor."

"Thank you." She flung a look to the broad-shouldered man barricading the door. "I have to go before he explodes with annoyance and his guts go flying everywhere."

Once again, Ishaq's laughter carried throughout the room. "Have a good night."

"You, too."

Grabbing her bag, she tried to avoid dragging her feet as she followed Akin out. What did this night hold in store?

CHAPTER TEN

Akin dreaded the time he'd be alone with Comfort. Not after the ass he'd made of himself in the sickbay. Jealousy had grabbed him by the balls and twisted. Hard. What did he have to be jealous of? She wasn't his woman. Hell, he couldn't even see them together.

The lie scraped like claws across his brain as even now, the need to grasp her full, rounded hips and hold her flush against him tempted. Okay, so he wanted her sexually. Like most of the other sailors, he hadn't been successful with his first marriage. After two years of being married to a military man, his ex-wife had hounded him to leave the navy so they could start a family. Removing an appendage would've been easier than exiting the navy. It was his life. Then and now.

The realization that he'd already been married to the navy before ever meeting his ex-wife had hit him hard. After a year of pleading, she'd given up and asked him to file for a divorce. He'd been heartbroken over losing the woman he thought he'd spend the rest of his life with, yet relieved because he hadn't had to let go of his first love.

As they entered the dining area, Akin became alert. The men didn't bother to be covert about looking at their resident doctor. One of them had the audacity to wave at her. He scowled harder when she returned the gesture.

Grabbing a tray, he shoved it in her direction. "You can't be too friendly with them."

Comfort's broad smile and enthusiastic hello to the server revealed what she thought about his order. Nothing.

She pointed to the char-grilled steak. Did the man give her the biggest piece in the pile? White rice was loaded onto her plate along with a tomato stew. When she scrunched her nose at the mixed vegetables, the attendant frowned, as if taking her displeasure personally.

"What's wrong?"

"I don't like carrots."

Tired of the scene, Akin lost his patience. "So pick them out."

The two ignored him. "What kind of vegetables do you like?"

What the hell?

"I eat them all, except carrots."

He nodded. "If you'll give me five minutes, I'll bring you some steamed green beans."

Another smile lit up her face. "You don't have to go through all that trouble for me."

"I insist."

She didn't have the chance to rebut because he'd scampered away to make her order, leaving Akin's plate empty.

"Hey," Akin barked.

The server returned. "Sorry, sir."

Although she had her head bowed, Comfort's shoulders shook with what he translated to be silent laughter. Her eyes had tears in them when she looked up.

"I see that you have a salad bar. I'll get something from over there instead of having the green beans. Thank you for the offer, though."

"Just let me know if you need anything, Doc."

"I will." She looked at his nametag, "Michael."

Jaw clenched and plate full, Akin followed her to get her salad and drinks before he found them a seat. After a few mouthfuls of food, Dubem plopped his tray next to Comfort's and took over the conversation that Akin hadn't had the chance to initiate.

Stabbing a fork into the tender meat, Akin focused on the meal. The indent of the cutlery's handle into his fingers as he clasped hard helped him to almost ignore the searing jealousy. For the second time in the same day, he wondered what the hell was wrong with him.

Why couldn't they sit in the cafeteria for the rest of the night chatting with Dubem? The man could charm mercy into a serial killer. He still had the moments of sharing random thoughts she'd witnessed when they'd been in The Gambia, but she'd learned to ignore it.

Why wasn't she attracted to him, then? Not that she was looking for someone, but anything would be better than fantasies of the giant Commander of Warfare moulding his lips to hers. Nipping her flesh until she moaned. Would his lips be as firm as he tended to hold them with his annoyed expressions, or would they be soft and yielding? His large hands stroking up and down her back. Dissolving her resolve to stay away from men while his mouth ravaged hers into supplication.

She snapped out of her illicit and unwarranted thoughts when Akin stood and grumbled.

"Since you're finished eating, let's go. You have some unpacking to do."

And just like that, she knew her romantic whims about him would never come to fruition. The man was too stern to ever put her at ease. If she were to fall for someone, he'd have to be able to protect her and make her laugh. Make her melt in his arms. He'd be enough to override the hell she'd been through within the past five years. Her light in the middle of a so far gruelling, debilitating tunnel. Basic communication on a friendly level, which Akin didn't possess, would be mandatory.

Not that she was looking for a man, she reminded herself once again, but he definitely wouldn't fit the bill. Akin's growls of agitation throughout dinner had to be the best part of the whole day. Served his mean arse right. He wasn't meant to be her lover, or even a friend, but she was sure she'd find him inadvertently entertaining for the rest of the mission. That's if he didn't aggravate her to the point of doing bodily harm.

Dubem got up and followed.

"What do you do for fun around here?" she asked as they made their way down the metallic passageway.

"Unpack our things and put them away in an orderly fashion," Akin responded.

Comfort curled her upper lip at his back. "I wasn't talking to you."

And then, she looked up into Dubem's perpetually twinkling eyes.

"What he said." Dubem's chuckle followed them as he took a right down the opposite passageway.

Through a hatch door, down a flight of stairs, and along the maze of passageways, they finally reached their room. For once, she was glad she'd be escorted everywhere—otherwise, she'd have to take the daily risk of getting lost. "How do you find your way so easily?"

"This is my ship."

She held back a sigh of frustration. "If I were to walk down these halls by myself—" she held up a hand when he pointed a finger at her and she rushed to add, "—which I won't, how could I avoid getting lost?"

His eyes darkened as his pupils grew wider with his narrowed gaze.

Comfort could see why his men feared him. She was sure he had the skills to back up his warnings. She refused to retreat from his threatening glower. "I promise, unless it's an emergency, you won't see me in the halls alone."

That's because I'll hide before you can catch a glimpse of me.

He waved at the sign on the wall with numbers and letters on it. "That will tell you everything you need to know."

"Looks like it could be used to test someone's eyesight."

One side of his face shifted upward. Was that a near smile?

"I'll teach you how to read it later. Right now, we both need to settle in and get some rest." He opened the door. "Tomorrow, we have PT—physical training—at zero five hundred."

A squeak escaped her throat at the sight of the sleeping area. She rotated her neck left and right searching for more space. It didn't appear. Four beds, two bunks on each side, took up most of the room, leaving a small walkway between the beds where a chair waited against the wall. The single cabin she'd declined took up more space than this area. At least there, she could stretch her arms to the sides and not touch metal without having to face a bed. Damn her fear. Damn her life.

She took consolation in the fact that she wouldn't be suffering alone. If she had liked him, she'd have felt sorry for Akin. Self-preservation won out over being able to spin in the room without whacking him. Had he grown larger since he'd stepped into the place?

He plucked up a pile of dark blue material from a bed and thrust it at her.

Knowing what she held, but not wanting to accept it, she held the load at arm's length. "What's this?"

"Your uniforms. No one stands out on this ship. Especially not you."

With her muscles getting tired, she pulled the uniforms closer. "The shortest person I've seen here still topped me by a few inches. I'll be swimming in these."

His sigh reminded her of a teacher dealing with a rather difficult child. It spiked her irritation.

"You can roll them up or tuck them into your boots."

Her brows rose. "Boots?"

He pointed to a way smaller pair than his sitting against the wall. The nastiness in his smirk stole some of his handsomeness. "Captain's orders."

Biting her lip, she glared at the wretched man. Did he live to make her life uncomfortable? A deep breath cleared her head the tiniest bit. After dealing with the men's flirting, she understood how things would go better for her if she were to appear less feminine. It wouldn't stop them from knowing she was one, but at least, her curves would be hidden.

"Choose a rack," he ordered.

"What?"

That damn half grin made a reappearance. This time making fun of her. "Your bunk."

Still standing at the door with her arms full, she tipped her head to indicate the room. "This place is so small. How can two people, never mind four, fit in here?"

"Very carefully with no sudden movements. And you have to be considerate."

She took offense. Was he referring to her decision not to sleep alone, dragging him down with her. "What does that mean, Commander?"

He raked a hand down his face. "Nothing."

She placed the uniforms on the bottom mattress to her right.

"It didn't sound like nothing." Taking her guilt and anger out on him, she poked him in the chest. "If you have something to say, Solarin, then say it."

With a calm that chilled the room, he took a step back. "Which rack do you want?"

Temper flaring, she stepped into his face again. "You don't know me or what I've been through. Don't you dare dismiss me like I'm one of your men. What did you mean?"

When he stood resolute, she whirled towards the door in an attempt to storm out. He caught her by the arm.

"Where the hell do you think you're going?"

Tugging herself from his grip, she continued towards the passageway. With the extension of his long limb, he closed the metal and kept her in all while swinging his body in front of hers to block the way.

The standoff continued with a stare-down. Every muscle in her body tautened with the tension. She couldn't maintain the stance all night, so she caved. "I'm going to the captain to change rooms. I can't stay here with you."

"Who would you rather have as a cabin mate? Dubem?"

The stress on the man's name took her aback. Was he jealous? She'd thought his behaviour at the Mess had been out of annoyance. The realization snatched the ire out of her. Her shoulders slumped as a deep sorrow took its place.

"No one."

His brows drew together. "But you refused the single."

His voice held no blame, only curiosity.

She was responsible for him leaving the comfort of his cabin only to be trapped in this tomb with her. She may as well be honest. What did she have to lose?

"I mean, I wish things were different and I didn't need to share a room with anyone. That I could be brave enough to sleep alone."

Suddenly exhausted, she shuffled to the chair and allowed gravity to sink her body into it, head thumping against the wall. She'd need the support to answer the questions she knew he wouldn't be able to resist asking.

CHAPTER ELEVEN

Comfort's pain tugged at him. Two long strides brought him to her. If he were a better person, he'd grab his things and start putting them away without interrogating her.

No one had ever called him good. Vicious, determined, hard, and focused were terms he'd heard used to describe him, even though they'd been said behind his back.

Kindness had never been his strong suit. Where had this need to hold her come from? He kept his hands to himself out of his own fear. Once he cradled her, would he ever want to stop?

Folding himself onto the edge of the bunk, he rested his elbows onto his thighs. "Whatever happened to you has had a serious impact on your life. If you'd like to share, then please do. Otherwise, we should put our things away."

He couldn't force her to engage.

Akin waited a full minute as she continued to lean her head against the wall with her eyes closed, her chest rising and falling in a rapid rhythm.

"Six years ago, I could sleep anywhere. I had finished my training as a general practitioner. Did my scheduled stints with the reserves. Had a huge family who I couldn't get enough of." She opened her eyes and looked into his. "And the man I had fallen in love with and married in medical school adored me."

He prevented his sharp intake of air from making a gasping noise at her confession. His chest tightened in disappointment. He refused to think about why. Of course a beautiful, intelligent—and from what he could tell when she dealt with others—kind-hearted woman would be married. But it didn't explain her traipsing around the world treating people with diseases which gave a near fatal diagnosis to a large percentage of those who contracted it.

"I was happy then." She drew her legs up so her heels rested on the edge of the chair and hugged her knees. Head on forearms, she fixed her gaze away from him. "I was the middle child of five. Two sets of twins. The boys were older than the girls. Each pair was close." She raised her head. "You'd think that would've left me feeling left out, but it was as if I was a triplet to each set. They always included me. My..." she paused. "...parents made sure of it."

"Would you like some water?"

Although her story, filled with people set in the past tense, would end in misery, her eyes were dry.

"Yes, please."

Akin grabbed his duffle bag, dug into the side, and pulled out a water bottle. "I'll be right back."

Maybe the time away would help loosen the grip of emotion in his chest. Never had he felt so distressed for someone other than his childhood self, and she hadn't even completed her story.

Hustling to the water fountain a short distance down the passageway, he filled the bottle. He greeted a few of the off-duty men as they passed, then returned to the cabin. A deep inhale fortified him with the strength he knew he'd need to endure her past.

Stepping inside, he went to her and handed her the drink.

"Thank you."

This time, he sat within reaching distance on the rack. His ex-wife had accused him on several occasions of not being demonstrative enough. He'd never felt the need to show his support with touch. Until now.

She took a few sips of the water, bent to the side, and settled the bottle on the floor. "My youngest brother, the most serious out of all of us—" her grim smile didn't reach her eyes, "—fell in love with a woman from Portugal. Of course, when they decided to get married, she wanted the wedding in her country so all her friends and family could be there." The words had been said with a hard bite to them. "My brother would've done anything for her, so that's where they arranged for the wedding.

"I think my parents were more excited than the couple. Not only was one of their children marrying a woman they liked, but they'd get to take a full family vacation. It had been years since we'd gone on one together."

The sound of her swallow filled the cabin. He clutched his hands together, struggling to tamp down the rising apprehension as he waited for the heart of the story to ram into him.

"The day before the wedding, my parents insisted on a family outing before we became extended once again. My brother's fiancée pitched a fit, but we told her it would happen with or without her blessing. Dad arranged for a vehicle to pick us up, and we went out for a family breakfast." This time, her grin crinkled the corners of her eyes. "We talked and laughed so much that I don't think any of us ate much of our food. It was one of the best days we've ever had together." Her eyes glazed over. "Until it wasn't."

Her skin indented where her fingers gripped her arms. "My brother's fiancée called him, demanding he return to the house to help deal with wedding preparations. We didn't want to leave the sanctuary of the day, but we knew we couldn't be selfish, either. On the way back, a torrential rainstorm hit." Her shoulders shimmied as if she'd become chilled. "A loud boom ricocheted through the vehicle, making it shake. All of a sudden, we were skidding out of control and then rolling."

She rubbed a hand against her scar and then down her face. Wrapping her arms around her legs, she rocked. Yet, still no tears.

"I woke up in a hospital room disoriented and alone. I screamed for my mother, but my voice came out hoarse as if I hadn't used it in a while. Fear the likes of nothing I had ever experienced claimed me. I struggled to get out of bed only to fall because my legs wouldn't hold me. A week in a coma turns your muscles to jelly."

Oh, God. His arms ached to hold her. Would she fight him or let him comfort her? They were strangers who'd met yesterday. What right did he have to want to shield her from her own pain? Instead, he balled his hands into tight fists and waited for the end.

"When the nurse came, she called for help, and they got me into bed. I asked them where my family was. No one would look at me. Somehow, I knew, but I remained optimistic."

How could she have gone through such loss and still survived?

"Finally, a priest came and gave me the news that everyone who'd been in the car, including the driver, had died. I'd gotten away with a severe head injury which they'd had to send me to surgery for. They'd almost given up hope that I'd wake up." The whites of her eyes were reddened, yet she hadn't shed a single tear as she held his gaze. "I wish I hadn't."

A hard lump formed in his throat, making it impossible to breathe. His eyes burned as if acid had been thrown into them. Then, he felt the wetness slide down his cheeks. They wouldn't stop no matter how hard he tried to make them. He swiped them away with the sleeve of his shirt.

She stood and reached out a hand to him. He grasped her lifeline, held her hand, and got up. Her arms around him was a balm; yet, the pain, that he felt on her behalf, remained. How could she stand to have lived all these years when she'd lost the people who had loved her most in the world? How was life fair?

It wasn't, and he knew it never would be.

He bit his lip and pulled out of her arms, mortified at his behaviour. She'd been the one who'd undergone the tragedy, not him. How had she ended up comforting him? A better question would be why had it affected him to the point of tears? He hadn't wept since he'd been a child. No one respected weakness. Crying didn't help the situation, so why bother?

He pivoted towards the door, giving her his back to compose himself. When he turned to look at her, she'd lifted her suitcase off the bed and onto the floor. She unzipped it and pulled out her clothes.

"Where can I stow my things?"

Humiliated at his emotional reaction, he grabbed the handle on the rack of the bottom bunk and lifted it with more force than necessary to expose the empty compartments beneath the mattress.

"You can have all three storage areas. I only need one," he said, his voice as firm as when doling out punishment to a recalcitrant soldier. He then went to put his things away.

"Sleeping became almost impossible," she said in a clear voice as if she hadn't told a story that had driven him to tears. "And whenever I did fall asleep and woke up alone, my loss would torment me. My husband hadn't been able to make it to the wedding, but he rushed down when they'd told him I was in a coma. A week later, I was back home in Brighton."

They put their things away in silence, staying out of each other's way as best they could in the miniscule space.

"I saw a psychiatrist for my depression, but I refused to be put on medication." She shrugged as if he'd asked a question. "I didn't think they'd help. Nine months later, my husband told me he'd be filing for a divorce because I was no longer the woman he'd married and he couldn't live as if the world had ended anymore."

A white, searing fury ravaged all thought as he gripped the cold metallic edge of the top rack. How could the man leave the woman he'd promised to love for the rest of his life instead of working it out?

You did, his mind teased. Or at least, he'd allowed it to happen without much of a fight.

Warmth seeped into his arm, and he looked down to see her hand touching him.

"It's okay. I've forgiven him." She removed her fingers, and the tingling which had ignited in the area faded. "He had every right to want to live a healthy life with someone who wasn't broken and petrified to sleep without him by her side."

"He should've stayed."

She cocked her head, her dark eyes piercing. "He did the right thing. I needed to learn how to live again. If he'd been around, I would've continued to wallow and would've eventually died from my grief."

Her words held a surety to them. Had she been thinking of committing suicide? He couldn't bring himself to ask.

She pointed towards her second suitcase. "Where can I keep this?"

"Don't you need anything from it?"

She shook her head. "Not now. I no longer have a home since I joined MSF, so I carry everything with me. Including my memorabilia."

"I'll send it to the storage room tomorrow."

He looked at his watch. Twenty-three hundred hours. Where the hell had the time gone? Down a rabbit hole where he'd lost his senses.

"We need to get some sleep." At least, he did. "Let me show you the head and showers. It's not far."

Back to himself, he levelled her with a stern look.

"I know. I know. I'm not to go anywhere by myself. A person would think you'd have loosened up after hearing my story."

"Is that what you want?"

What if she claimed yes? Despite his moment of weakness, it wasn't in him to go soft. On anybody. Another complaint his ex-wife had barraged him with.

Her eyes went wide. "Pity? Hell, no."

Neither did he. He wanted them to be the same as before she'd lain her heavy burden at his feet. "Then do as I say with no questions, and everything will be fine."

"Now you've gone crazy." She left the cabin and waited for him to join her.

He didn't doubt that he had.

CHAPTER TWELVE

After a quick shower, Comfort lay in her coffin of a bed. The royal blue curtain was drawn to keep the world out. Or at least, a big, brooding man who'd shed tears for her when she couldn't for herself.

She flipped onto her side and faced the wall. The man who could be the poster boy for alpha male of the decade with his gruff, hard, take-no-nonsense, give-no-nonsense exterior actually possessed a heart. One which had bled for her.

Afterward, his frustration at his unexpected reaction had lashed out at her, and she'd allowed it. After all, wasn't it her fault? She'd told him her story. Something she hadn't done since joining MSF. None of the people she'd shared accommodations with over the years or worked closely with to save lives knew the burden she carried.

She flipped onto her back with a sigh. The years had lessened the pain, but it still resided within her. Night-time was the hardest. With others in the world able to sleep without a problem, the haunting memories of her family kept her awake. Filling her with loneliness, regret, and most of all guilt.

Why had she survived and they'd died? The question plagued her, and no one had been able to answer with anything but platitudes.

She did a one-eighty roll onto her stomach and landed with a plop on the hard mattress. She could see why Ishaq preferred the bed in the sick bay. Maybe she should check on him. It would be worth annoying her protector. A quick glance at the e-reader she'd ignored for the past hour revealed the time to be two in the morning.

Raising her head, she adjusted the pillow and then willed herself to sleep. A self-deprecating snort escaped.

She'd relived the horror of her past tonight. The best she could hope for was an hour of unconsciousness, if that.

Akin must think her cold and unfeeling at her lack of emotion when telling her tale.

What did his opinion matter?

A lot. She respected him. He knew his mission in life. To be the best naval officer he could be. She envied that. She also wanted to know her purpose. Instead, she roamed around the world attempting to help others as a way to escape living her own life.

She picked up her e-reader to stop her mind from the aimless thinking. The non-fiction about leadership didn't hold her interest for even one sentence before she laid it back down.

What did Akin say they were doing early in the morning? PT? What did it entail? Hopefully, no jogging would be involved. Or pushups.

Comfort rolled onto her side and pulled her curtain apart the slightest bit. Expecting to see blue curtains on the opposite bed, she jumped a little to see Akin's body outlined in the light from her rack. Lying on his back, he'd flung his arm over his forehead. She watched as his flat abdomen rose and fell with each breath.

What would it be like to be so at peace that she could just sleep? She let her gaze roam from the top of his head down his wide muscular chest covered in a dark T-shirt. He'd draped a blanket over his lower body. No one would disagree with her about him being a powerful man. A breath-stealing handsome one, at that.

She should close her curtain and struggle to get some sleep.

Try as she might, her arm refused to obey the mental order.

Watching him relaxed her. She synced her breath to his as she stared at the parts of his profile not covered by his corded forearm. His nose took on a longer slope from the side, and the broadness of his chin wasn't as prominent.

Those lips remained the same. What would they feel like against her tongue as she tasted him?

Her breaths came too quickly, and she returned to mimicking his pattern. Rhythmic and calming. Abdomen rising up and down. Air flowing in and out. Her eyes drifted closed.

Akin turned his head to the side and opened his lids. She'd finally fallen asleep, her upper body so close to the edge, he feared she'd fall out. He didn't dare move her or turn off her rack light. She'd struggled for this moment of rest. Her tossing and turning every few moments had kept him awake and alert to her unease.

Concerned, he'd argued with himself on whether to give up pretending to sleep and talk to her. He'd been about to speak when her light had pierced his lids. She hadn't spoken, yet, he'd felt her attention on him, and after a few moments when he'd expected her to change position, nothing had happened.

And then, her soft snores had reached his ears. He wouldn't do anything to disturb the sleeping woman. Not even kiss her on the ragged scar exposed to him. If only the press of his lips could take away or at least diminish the torment she'd been through.

It couldn't. Nothing would.

He turned his body to lie on his side facing her and forced himself to close his eyes. The image of her beautiful face and sad, yet dry eyes never left him.

After everything she'd been through, she deserved to feel as if she were no longer alone in the world. For the short time they'd be acquainted, he'd be that for her. Her protector. Her safety net. The person she could count on not to leave her.

Until *she* left *him* at the end of the mission.

The thought of her not being around had him digging his nails into his palms as he balled his fists.

He relaxed and dragged the blanket up to his shoulders. For the time they'd be together, he'd try his damnedest to make sure she knew peace. He had no idea how he'd accomplish the task, but he'd set his mind to it and would make it happen. Maybe if he guided her towards it, he'd also find it himself.

CHAPTER THIRTEEN

"Wake up."

Comfort curled herself into a ball as she attempted to ignore the deep voice intruding into her sleep.

"It's time for PT," the voice insisted.

Who needed exercise when she could get more delicious rest? And then, her eyes sprang open to find a pair of thick, muscular legs blocking her view of anything else.

She wasn't in The Gambia. She'd landed herself a job as a ship's doctor on an international naval vessel.

She flopped onto her back. Squeezing her eyes closed, she remembered what had happened last night. Maybe if she started to snore, he'd leave her alone.

"Get up, Princess. Time to exercise. It's mandatory for everyone on my team."

Princess? Was he making fun of her?

"What?" She smacked her lips together in an attempt to get rid of the cottony dryness. "I'm not on your team. Sick bay is under Logistics, remember?" As much as she didn't like the man, she had to play the rank card. "Commander Deyma Lewis owns my arse."

Holding back a groan at the way her words sounded to her own ears, she opened her eyes and tried again. "I'm not navy. Civilian all the way. I don't belong to anyone."

He squatted so his face took up her peripheral vision. "You're under my protection. You're mine."

Her stomach did convoluted things as she turned her head to be struck by the intensity in his eyes. Why did he have to look so good in the morning?

"Besides," he continued. "This is a combat vessel. I'm the Commander of Warfare. Everyone is my responsibility, and I make it my duty to ensure that each person trains at least once a week while we're at sea."

He couldn't boss everyone around. She hoped her grin expressed how much she was gloating inside. "Even the captain?"

"*Especially* the captain." He'd knocked her down with those three words. "Now get up, or you'll do extra pushups for making me late."

"Fine," she grumbled as she swung her legs over the side of the bed.

"Be careful of your head."

His warning came just before she flung her body upward. She took her time rising so she didn't knock her head against the low-lying top rack. Bent in half on the bed, she glared up at him. "What if I don't have workout clothes?"

"I'd be shocked. A woman as toned as you must exercise."

Had he just complimented her? Her face filled with heat.

Standing, she avoided his gaze. "I'll be ready in five minutes."

"Make it four."

She bit her tongue and got to hustling, grabbing her workout gear and toothbrush. "I'm going to the head."

He nodded and stepped in front of her to lead the way.

She'd never get accustomed to being treated like protected royalty. Absolutely never.

Akin rushed Comfort up the stairs to the area he'd designated for their training. About fifty of the men had assembled, including Captain Obot. Akin paused to raise an I-told-you-so brow at his cabin mate. She stuck her nose into the air and turned her gaze towards the sea.

A group jog around the upper deck and empty helicopter hangar, calisthenics, and stretches completed their warm up. Today, he'd focus on hand-to-hand combat. They'd never had to use it, but he wanted to ensure that the men were able to if necessary. He'd also concentrate on teaching Comfort skills to protect herself. Not that he'd allow anyone past him in order to reach her, but training her would allow him to have some peace of mind. Just in case.

He taught his men to fight dirty, just as he'd learned from one of the meanest instructors at boot camp. Of course, he'd had to request to join the man's training and had been physically tortured with endurance exercises in order to prove himself worthy. Although he'd trained with more civilized styles of martial arts later in life, he'd never forgotten what mattered most. Surviving by any means necessary.

"Grab a mat and partner up." To his annoyance, many of the men clamoured to Comfort. "Djan, you're with me."

Audible groans could be heard on the deck, including hers.

When the men formed a semi-circle around him, he projected his voice. "As I've mentioned before, most of self-defence is awareness and anticipation. If you can avoid a strike, do. If you can't, then recover and get out causing as much damage as possible. Today, we're working on close-range weapon strikes."

He pulled out a blunted knife from a box he'd asked one of the men to bring over. "Fallou."

"Sir."

The man had been ready in the front row. Being tall, lean, and fast on his feet made him the perfect partner to demonstrate with.

"Attack me with this knife."

Akin bent his knees and kept his weight light as they circled each other. Fallou made a slashing motion with the weapon, which Akin easily circumvented with a quick jump backwards.

When his attacker came in straight towards his abdomen, Akin stepped to the side. The blade missed as he blocked with one hand headed upward and the other one down, protecting his body. The hand pointing skyward flashed down and grabbed Fallou's wrist. An elbow to the armpit deadened the knife-wielding arm. The weapon dropped to the floor. Akin struck at Fallou's elbow with his forearm, which would've broken his opponent if he'd made contact. Twisting the arm, he applied pressure to it behind Fallou's back until he tapped.

Akin released him. "Keep it simple. The point is to not get cut while unarming your opponent."

He went through the movements step by step before telling them to grab a knife and practice.

Comfort stood to the side, watching him. What was she thinking? Would she be willing to train? As if he'd give her a choice.

"Come here."

Her unscarred brow arched.

"Please," he added.

The grin and bounce in her step as she walked had him hiding his own amusement by wiping a hand down the lower half of his face.

"Do you need me to break down what I just went through again?"

"No."

"I'm going to attack you."

She rolled her eyes. "I'm pretty sure an assailant wouldn't be informing me of his actions."

He looked for an opportunity to come in as she assumed the same stance he had during the demonstration. Circling each other, he jabbed at her. Her movements were a blur as she subdued him with moves he hadn't demonstrated to the crew. The next thing he knew, he lay face down on the mat, both arms behind his back with her attempting to break them. He tapped out with his foot.

Jumping off of him, she reached a hand down to assist him up.

Ignoring her, he stood on his own, shaking out his arms. "I took it easy on you."

Her shrug and neutral expression should've been his clue that her pin had nothing to do with luck. Pride wouldn't let him admit it.

Once again with the knife in hand, he circled her. Faking a straight jab, at the last moment, he lunged to the side and swiped his hand in order to slice her abdomen. She dodged the first jab and rather than block the swipe with her hands, she rotated around him until she faced him from the other side. His arm out, he stood wide open.

She spun and landed a side kick to his chest, making him stumble backward with a loud grunt. Her eyes brightened as she became the attacker. An inside kick to his knife-wielding arm sent the weapon flying when his arm went numb. Her hands became fuzzy with their speed as two strikes to the side of his neck landed with a soft touch. She'd held back. The strikes would've sent him to his knees if she'd made full contact.

Quick as lightning, another side kick headed towards his head when she shifted away from him. He'd gained his wits and stepped towards her to block it with raised forearms. He'd pay for the pain of bone on bone later. He didn't doubt she would, too.

She put her foot down and leapt away from him with her hands still in guard position to protect her head. His men went wild with their cheering. Pushing his pride to the side, he nodded his approval. "Get back to practicing."

He rubbed his chest where her heel hadn't hesitated to make contact. "What the hell was that?"

"Black belt. Third degree. Specialty is hand to hand." She reached up and brushed a palm over her hair to smooth down the ponytail. "I learned in the reserves that I'm an okay shot, but I can incapacitate an attacker no matter their size." She held up hands which she used to heal as a profession. "Two if the situation demands."

"Show me."

Her brows puckered, creating an indent in the middle of her forehead. "Are you sure? I don't want to hurt anyone. I don't have as much control when it comes to multiple attackers."

Already proud as hell for her defence against him, he wanted to see if she could back up her claim. "Stay away from knees, groins, eyes, ears, and throats, and everyone'll be fine."

She stuck out her bottom lip. "But those are my favourites."

He chuckled at her fake whine, resisting the urge to stroke his tongue along the slit of her mouth. He turned to the men who'd been watching them. "I need two volunteers."

He didn't have to ask again before they ran up. The others gathered around, leaving a ring of space. "You'll attack the doctor with grabs, punches, kicks, whatever you need to in order to subdue her. Treat her as if she were the enemy. If you hold back, you'll have to deal with me. Is that understood?"

"Yes, sir," the duo agreed as excitement buzzed through the group.

Akin stepped back, rubbing his hands together with anticipation, the deeper meaning of the demonstration not lost on either him or his men. If she could defeat these two men, only the fools on this ship would dare try to take advantage of her. They'd meet the floor before they could even think to try.

"Fight!"

CHAPTER FOURTEEN

"I heard you kicked ass in PT." Ishaq, fully dressed in uniform, spoke from the desk instead of his bed or the chair next to it when she limped into the sick bay. "Started with two, and when you took them down, Akin challenged you with another one until all three lay groaning on the mats."

Once they'd learned she hit for real, so had they. Already, her muscles had started protesting, and her shin was forming a bruise. She wiggled the jaw where one of the meaty-fisted guys had clipped her. The right kidney punch and tackle to the ground where she'd landed on her back and had had to fight her way up hadn't tickled, either.

Akin's grin at the end of the bout indicated how proud he was of her. She might take on another set just to see that smile aimed at her again.

"You should be in bed," she chastised Ishaq.

Hell, so should she.

"Is it true that the last guy refused to volunteer? He had to be drafted after seeing what you did to the other two?"

"No comment. I know you aren't planning to work for even half of the day. I need you to recover."

He ignored her advice. "Where did you learn to fight so fiercely?"

"A fight club in downtown London."

Ishaq's eyes went round. "Really?"

Laughing hurt her jaw and her stomach, which had taken a blow. "No. When my older brothers started karate, I tagged along."

"How old were you?"

Foreseeing an interrogation, she eased herself into the seat adjacent to him "Ten."

"Have you been training all these years?"

She hitched a shoulder. Mistake. "Off and on. Mostly on."

It had helped her maintain her sanity when she'd been on the cusp of losing it after her family died.

Ishaq picked up a pen and tapped it against the desk. "Even while you've been with MSF?"

"I had a couple of people on every team that I'd train with when we had time."

He slid a folder in her direction. "I bet your brothers can take you out."

Her skin prickled. She may as well get it out the way.

"They stopped a year after they started. But they're dead now." Holding his gaze, she continued with her admission. "My whole immediate family is gone. I'm the last."

Her chest didn't tighten as much as it normally did at the admission.

The darkness of his eyes softened. "You have my condolences."

As a medical professional, he must've seen his share of death. Even if he were curious about the how of her loss, he wouldn't ask. If she decided to volunteer the information, she knew he'd listen.

"Thank you. I'm going to start work." She pointed a warning finger at him. "When you need to rest, go. Ancille and I—" How could she have missed that they were missing a staff member? "Where is Ancille?"

Ishaq tipped his chin towards the door. "I sent him to get some ice."

"For what?"

He broke out into a grin. "You. There's no way you won't need it after what Akin put you through today."

About to give a sarcastic comment, she realized he'd called the commander by his first name. "Why do you call him Akin instead of Solarin?"

"When you enter the navy together, become as close as brothers, and rise through the ranks at the same pace, you earn the right to forgo the formality. If someone were around, you'd hear me call him by his last name."

The memory of Akin hovering over Ishaq in the Emergency Room floated into her mind. "What's your rank?"

He chuckled and glanced down at his arm. "I'll forgive you for not recognizing our rank insignias, Army. I'm a commander."

"In my defence, I'm a little dizzy. I've never once seen you in a uniform until today." She really should've known. Although gentler in nature, he possessed a domineering presence. Her mind overflowed with curiosity. She asked one last question, banking the rest for later. "How long have you been in service?"

"In a few months, it'll be twenty years. I'm up for retirement this year."

She broke her own promise of no more questions. "Will you take it?"

He rubbed the muscles at the back of his neck and smirked. "My wife hasn't given me a choice in the matter. And I think it's time. I've served with honour for my country."

Would Akin ever give up roaming on the sea to settle down?

None of her business—she'd never discover the answer. Her stomach plummeted with disappointment.

***

Comfort set her lunch tray on the table and waited for Akin to sit. "How far are we from Nigeria?"

He glanced up at her before turning his attention to his food and shovelling a chunk of chicken breast into his mouth.

Figuring she wouldn't get an answer until he was good and ready to give her one, she started in on her own meal.

She scrunched her nose at a familiar, overused cologne. The punk who'd outright propositioned her sank into the seat to her left. She ignored Umale as he joined the conversation with the others.

Akin indicated towards the drinks and raised his brows. She declined with a shake of the head. When he left the table, Umale closed enough of the space between them to not appear suspicious.

"Solarin shouldn't be the only one screwing you," he said in a voice that didn't carry to anyone else at the table as they joked and laughed. "I'm sure I could give it to you better and harder than the old man."

His smile freaked her out almost as much as him placing a hand on her knee and sliding it upward.

She'd gone beyond shocked to livid as soon as the crude words had left his mouth. Yet, she wasn't willing to cause this man's death at Akin's hand. Because her protector would kill him. Or attempt to until six men pulled him off the bastard.

She looked Umale in the eyes, placed her hand on his upper thigh, and slid it towards the inside seam. He licked his lips as if anticipating something tasty. She then pinched the sensitive skin of his inner thigh as hard as she could. Just as she'd intended, the pain registered even through the uniform material. His squeal as he attempted to jump from his seat only to be stopped by the heavy table had everyone looking at him.

She angled her head to view him from the corner of her eye. "Are you all right?"

His light skin flushed bright, and his nostrils flared with frustrated anger as his top lip curled. The expression spoke of danger and retribution. She gripped her fingers over her knife.

"Um, I got a leg cramp," he answered as his eyes threw daggers at her.

"Remember to drink lots of water," she advised without her voice shaking with disgust. "We had a tough workout this morning, even though I didn't see you there."

Akin returned to the table just as one of the guys picked up her lead and told him about the beating she'd handed out to both Akin and the three men while taking hits herself.

Blood drained from Umale's face at the telling of the morning PT session. It still didn't erase her need to shower after his illicit words and touch made her feel as if slime had been oozed over her. Damn men who thought they were God's gift to women. Double damn men who thought they had the right to overpower her when they absolutely didn't.

She pushed the rest of her meal away, unable to finish the now tasteless roasted chicken.

She stood when Akin did. Time to get back to work when she'd rather curl up in a ball on her bed with the door locked after the hottest shower the water heater could produce.

Outside the Mess, instead of taking a left towards sick bay as she'd expected, they went in the opposite direction.

"I want to show you something before we return to work."

They took the metal stairwell up until she squinted as the bright sun shone on them. The wind snagged a few strands of hair from her ponytail into her face.

They walked past where they'd trained that morning. Sailors went about their daily grind, never lacking for things to do.

"What's wrong?" Akin asked.

She blinked up at him.

"Nothing," she lied.

He studied her for an uncomfortably long time until she turned towards the sea.

He kept his focus on her. "You were quiet at lunch when I returned. You tend to chatter like a parrot during meals. I've only eaten a few times with you, but you've never left food on your plate before. Today, you did."

She tucked her lips into her mouth, incredulous that he'd noticed those things about her. She should report

Umale to him, but wouldn't. If the man hadn't learned his lesson from her blatant, painful rejection, then the stories of what she was capable of would straighten him out. Akin would probably throw him into the brig and make him starve for being so daring to someone under his protection. She had no desire to take the risk.

"I'm fine, thanks." She even smiled to placate him. "How many sailors are on board?"

He nodded with his lips in a tight line as if he didn't believe her, but answered. "Two hundred and five."

Without warning, he reached out and tucked a tendril of errant hair behind her ear. He stroked the back of his fingers down her jaw, inducing tingles over every inch he came in contact with.

"You have a bruise."

Why in the world wasn't she swatting him away? Unlike Umale's touch, Akin's made her want more.

"Consequence of not blocking or getting out of the way fast enough."

He let his hand drop, leaving the coolness of the wind to replace the heat he'd created. An honest smile spread over his face and crinkled the corners of his eyes. The delicious flutters in her belly threatened to double her over while basking in his presence.

"You impressed me with your skills this morning. Especially the way you took me down without breaking a sweat."

Was this what he'd brought her here to say? With no witnesses to prove that he'd actually given a compliment?

"Serves you right."

The condescending arch of his brow made an appearance. "For trying to teach you how to defend yourself?"

"No. For letting your guard down because you thought I didn't know what I was doing. It's a mistake many people make. And not only when it comes to self-defence."

His firm, dusky pink lips actually paled when he pressed them together. "Point taken."

He started walking, returning the salute of an armed sailor who'd reached them and then went about his duty.

They reached the back of the ship. He ran his hand over grooved areas of the metal railing which protected them from falling in.

Nothing but the vast sea before them. She had no idea how far they'd sailed, but she'd never been to the point where she couldn't see land. She liked it. All of it. The camaraderie amongst the men. The idea of being part of something great and meaningful. She could do without some of the harsh looks from a few of the men who still didn't want her on board, and Umale could feed himself to the sharks.

Akin turned to her and finally spoke. "I don't know how much longer we'll be at sea. It depends on what we encounter. Hopefully, nothing, and we'll have you disembarking in no time."

Was he in a rush to get rid of her?

"Oh, okay."

Could her tone have sounded any more dejected?

"It's nothing personal, but I didn't want you here in the first place."

Her heart sank. Well, that made things clearer. "I figured that with all the scowling, you were overjoyed."

He ignored her sarcasm.

"This is not a safe place for you. Pirates are greedy and brutal. Nigeria alone loses billions of dollars each year to oil theft. They kidnap crew members to take as hostages." He slammed the bottom of his fist against the rail. "The things they do to the women they capture would have you diving into the water to get away from the possibility of the danger you could face. Whoever they find useless in their endeavours, they kill. It's an organized crime that pays. Our mission is to protect these waters."

Her hands became clammy despite the breeze. "You sound like a news report."

His mighty shoulders rose and fell. "Facts are facts. Governments of West Africa were tired of losing all of that money, so they created WASPA."

A chill ran down her spine, making her shiver at people's greed and brutality. Long before she'd become a doctor, she'd wondered how people could be so cruel to each other. The question had risen to crescendo levels once she'd started working with MSF and entered war-torn areas where many were left to die at the hands of those more powerful. Unable to grasp how anyone could be so vicious to other human beings, she'd stopped trying to figure it out.

"Are you cold?"

He'd noticed her slight shiver?

"No. I just don't understand people."

His lips turned down into a grimace. "Abject poverty will drive a person do things they never thought they would."

She studied his sullen expression. "Do you have personal experience?"

As if snapping himself out of where his mind had travelled to, he stood straight. "We need to get back to work."

He'd closed himself off again. Why did it disturb her? Why should she care if he didn't share? They'd been thrown together because of the greed and callousness of others.

The memory of the tears of empathy he'd shed last night refused to leave her. Although she didn't want to know more about him or even like him as a person, she knew it was too late. It didn't mean she'd let him in as anything more than a colleague. She couldn't afford to.

CHAPTER FIFTEEN

Listening to the crew's problems took up the majority of Comfort's responsibility as ship's doctor. The most exciting medical event of the day included suturing a sailor who'd bumped his head.

"For some reason, someone hitting their head on some structure or another occurs on a daily basis," Ancille had informed her.

She'd been confused. "The ship is still. I don't even feel the waves."

Ancille had shrugged. "So it seems. It's a weird phenomenon. They move around a lot and don't always pay attention to where they're going. The equipment and tubing hanging in the passageways at all height levels don't help, plus it's not always so calm on the water. Let's hope we get back without having to deal with any storms."

Even with the steady stream of work that afternoon, thoughts of Akin kept intruding. The gentleness of his fingers sliding along her cheek. His smile which had competed with the sun. The way he'd actually give her information when she'd asked.

How many times had she shaken him out of her mind, only for him to boomerang in again? She wished he'd revert to his gruff self. Not the kind man who made her heart skip a beat.

Umale's disturbing actions at lunch hadn't strayed far from her mind, either. She struggled with telling Akin, settling on letting her protector know if something similar happened again. She'd been told that the men on board were the best of the best; she could only hope Umale had more common sense than he'd displayed so far.

By the time seven rolled around, Ishaq had gone to his cabin hours prior. It had taken some prodding and threats of having him carried out, with a few insults about him being a bad patient, but he'd finally gone.

Gideon came to relieve them of their twelve-hour shift. When Ishaq became well enough, they'd share a twelve-hour rotation and be on constant call. They'd most likely dock in Nigeria before then.

She and Ancille gave their brief report of the day to Gideon.

"Commander Solarin told me to escort you to the Mess and then to your berthing."

Had something happened to Akin?

"Why?"

She realized as soon as the word came out that she'd get no answer. Akin wouldn't have given an explanation for his order.

"Never mind." She recanted.

No alarms blaring or men rushing helter skelter meant the ship was neither under attack or attacking. Those were the two things which should worry her, not Akin's whereabouts. He was none of her business, whereas she'd been forced to be his.

It didn't stop her from being disappointed at not seeing him. *Dammit.* She shouldn't be feeling anything for him.

Grabbing her bag, she smiled at Gideon.

"Have a good night." Just as she had yesterday, she added, "Don't hesitate to call if you need me."

She and Ancille took off for the Mess where she'd fill her stomach. Maybe she'd even decompress by watching a mindless movie on one of the plasma screen televisions in one of the lounging areas of the berthing. By the time she got to the cabin, she'd be ready for a shower and then bed.

Would Akin be there waiting for her?

And then, she remembered she shouldn't care.

Akin attempted to be as silent as a thief when he stepped into his temporary lodgings. He kept the overhead light off as the tempting scent of flowers hit him. Without thought, he inhaled deeply, savouring the femininity of the woman he'd sleep beside, but never touch while she remained in his care. Pure torture.

He'd lost himself in her while on deck that afternoon. The loose strands of her hair blowing in the wind, the attention she'd showered on him, and the beauty she resonated had overwhelmed him. He'd stroked her jaw without thinking. Hoping to soothe the bruise which had formed. Huge mistake. He'd desired more after caressing the silky-smooth skin.

To pull the rest of her hair out of its confines and run his fingers through it. Holding her head still as he slid his lips along hers. Relishing their taste as he ignored their reality, bringing her nothing but pleasure.

Unwarranted desire had turned him into a coward. He'd stayed away from her this evening in an attempt to gain equilibrium. Logic dictated that if they didn't spend time together, maybe he wouldn't want her. So far, he'd been wrong.

She'd been upset while they'd been on the deck after lunch, yet hadn't wanted to share. He held back from prodding. If she ever wanted to tell him, she would. Then, he'd destroy whatever or whoever had troubled her. He only wished he could ease the pain of her past.

Her rack's closed curtain kept her from view. If he were lucky, she'd fallen asleep. After a quick change into a pair of shorts and a T-shirt, he crawled into his bunk. He held a mental debate about whether to leave his curtain open or not. Being able to see him last night seemed to have helped her settle into sleep.

A sudden change in position from his neighbour ended his indecision.

Exhausted on all levels, he attempted to put away his thoughts about training his men to be battle-ready, strategies, and the heaviness of the responsibility weighing on him of having to help keep so many safe.

He'd been trained to carry the burden.

A dim light made its presence known behind his closed lids. Taking deep, slow breaths, he simulated sleep although his heart raced. He waited, listening for Comfort to get out of bed to walk around or perhaps wake him to go to the head.

After a few minutes, a light snore reached his ears. Just as he had last night, he turned his head to find her facing him with her eyes closed. It hadn't taken her as long to fall asleep, and a deep pride filled him that he'd been able to help her. Either from the muscle-draining workout she'd received this morning or by her not being alone in the room, he couldn't tell. Just as long as she fell into a state of peace.

She deserved it.

"Sleep tight, Princess," he whispered.

He'd called her the endearment earlier in the day, and she hadn't reacted. The oddest part was that it had slipped so naturally from his mouth.

With Comfort now in dreamland, his eyelids drooped. Tomorrow would be soon enough to ensure everyone's continued safety. Especially hers.

CHAPTER SIXTEEN

Dubem strode into the sick bay, dimples displayed with his smile, and greeted.

Comfort's mouth responded in kind to the contagious gesture as she addressed him. "Good evening. Are you reporting to the clinic?"

He shook his head with an uncharacteristic frown. "Definitely not. I'm fitter than I've ever been."

With his tall, muscular frame and bright hazel eyes, she didn't doubt it. "What brings you here?"

"You. I'm your escort back to your cabin and wherever else you'd like to find yourself this evening."

Of their own accord, her shoulders drooped before she hitched them back up, refusing to be disappointed that Akin hadn't come for her. Yet again.

Two days had passed without seeing him. At least, not while he'd been awake.

Each night, he'd come in and settle into his bed as she lay still as a rock behind her curtain in an imitation of sleep. Silent and deep, even breathing would prevail for about ten minutes before she'd part the material and get her fill of him without his awareness. Before long, her eyes would drift closed, and she'd be lost to the world of the conscious.

Watching his chest rise and fall in a soothing rhythm as he slept ended up being better than hot chocolate topped up with two shots of rum and a bedtime story while cradled against a warm body in helping her to fall asleep.

His ability to act as a potent sleeping aid for her didn't detract from the disappointment which had settled into her gut. The bastard had ditched her, pawning his escort duties to others. What did he have to hide from when it came to her? Shouldn't she be the one trying to get out of his hovering presence? She had so much to lose. The more she got to know about him, the more she liked. Not a good thing considering that everyone she'd ever been connected to had left her.

Dubem tapped a finger to her nose. "I'm not that bad to be around, am I?"

Surprised by his touch, she stepped back and willed herself not to swat at him. It had only been a friendly gesture to grab her attention.

"Not at all." She turned to gather her things and said goodbye to Ancille. "I'm ready."

He opened the door and allowed her to exit first. A gentleman. Akin always breezed through the door, expecting her to follow. Another reason Dubem should be more attractive to her, yet he wasn't.

"How's your day been?" he asked.

She smiled at the gentle question. "It was good. We had a steady flow of men come in so it didn't get boring. How was yours?"

The heat from his hand at her lower back as he steered her around the corner made her want to shift away. This was a gentlemanly act she didn't appreciate. Not wanting to offend him when he didn't release her, she stopped, crouched, and pretended to tie the laces of her boot.

"It was okay. Better now, though," he said. "Never a dull moment on this ship, especially with you on board."

She glanced up to find him closer than he'd been a moment ago, with his bulging crotch at eye level. She stood so fast, she got dizzy and stumbled back.

He caught her by the shoulders. "Are you okay?"

She gained her balance. "Yes. Thank you."

Instead of letting her go, he squeezed her and rubbed his palms down her uniform-covered arms. His brandy-coloured eyes darkened as he lowered his head towards hers. She rotated her upper body, ducking her head and shoulders under his arm. She'd escaped his attempt at a kiss. Barely.

What the hell was going on?

"Akin is a lucky man to have you in his bed."

Dubem's voice had hardened to a point where she wouldn't have been able to associate it with him.

Comfort stopped walking and cricked her neck to look into his eyes, ready to blast him into last week for his presumption that she and Akin were sleeping together.

Before she could strangle out her words of reproach, he chuckled, rubbed the back of his neck, and kicked at the floor. "It really was a long day. I meant to say his berthing."

She assessed him from the side of her eye. Had he really just been about to kiss her, or had it been her imagination? And his word slip could've been accidental. Twelve-hour work days were no joke. He'd been nothing but kind to her, and other than the tone of his voice just then, she'd had nothing to fear from him.

"Akin is an upright man," he said when she didn't respond. "I'm sure he's taking good care of you by fulfilling all of your needs."

Why was she now reading things into everything he said? Maybe she'd been more affected by sharing her story of loss with Akin than she'd thought and was imagining things that weren't there.

Or maybe they're present, and you're just denying it.

She decided to pay attention to that little voice, but kept her mouth shut and continued walking towards her cabin.

Akin had said Dubem was one the few men he trusted. Although she and Akin didn't always get along, her gut told her that he was as honourable a man as he seemed to be. Dubem, on the other hand, was starting to show his true colours. They could never be hidden for long.

"I couldn't have had a better protector," she said. "He's been an absolute gentleman where it counts most."

"How are you enjoying your duty on the ship?"

She preferred the change of topic, but kept her internal guard up. He wouldn't have her questioning herself again.

What she'd experienced during their walk had been the truth of who he was, not the charming façade he put up.

"It's been a once in a lifetime experience."

He chuckled. "I'm sure it has. You have your pick of any man on the ship."

The comment had been more overt than the others. This time, she wouldn't let it slide. The impact was lost as she waited until two sailors passed by. "I don't want any man."

He raised a brow. "Just Akin, then?"

Her fingers flexed and extended, wishing his thick neck were between her hands and oxygen was being restricted from his body.

"How dare you?" The words came out hard. "That's the second time you've alluded to me and Akin being more than cabin mates. That's all we are, and I won't allow you to insinuate otherwise."

She did her best to level him with a stern glare from over a foot below him. "Do you understand, Commander Nzeogwu?"

She may have butchered his last name, but she'd just as soon shoot him in the abdomen than call him by his first name again.

He tipped his head "I do. Please know that if you need anything, I'm available, ready, and eager."

Hadn't he heard a word she'd spat at him? The man was incredible. He'd done it yet again without really saying anything wrong. He was a master word manipulator. She couldn't compete. She shouldn't have to.

Just so he'd be clear about the answer to his offer, she squinted up at him. "This ship will sink before that happens."

His grin didn't reach his eyes, which no longer sparkled. "*Reckoning* is a strong vessel. That's a no, then." He winked. "Sometimes, things have a way of changing."

Too close to hitting him with a right hook, Comfort stormed ahead of him towards the direction of her room.

"Comfort." His use of her first name grated. "Your cabin is to the left."

Grinding her teeth at her poor sense of direction, she pivoted back to where he stood and relented to have him lead her. This would be the last time they'd ever be alone together. Akin would fulfil his responsibility to her and keep her safe from any and all arseholes on the ship, whether he liked her or not.

She hadn't been able to work up the courage to have that long-needed chat about his abandonment when he'd arrived last night. He'd sounded so exhausted with his light grunts and sighs that she hadn't wanted to be an added problem to his day. So just like the nights prior, she'd watched him sleep.

Besides, as tired as he seemed, maybe he did have too much work to attend to that escorting her everywhere had become an added burden. He'd done as he'd said and sent someone so she'd never be alone.

A twisted nightmare of the crash had her struggling to wake up in the middle of the night. It had been Umale, Dubem, and her ex-boyfriend, not the heavy rainfall which had caused them being lifted and thrown off a bridge.

Panting, she flung her eyes open and searched for any sign of life. When she saw Akin kneeling at her bedside, the air flowed easily into her lungs.

"It was just a dream," he crooned in a gentle voice, caressing her forehead lighter than the touch of a feather. "You're safe in your bunk."

Safe with him. She held out her hand, needing the connection. He didn't hesitate to engulf her smaller hand in his larger, capable one. He'd reached his other hand out and rubbed her back as she lay on her side facing him.

Peace eased into her. Her lids became heavy as his rhythmic touch lulled her into a state of relaxation. A short while later, she fell asleep.

He'd left before she'd woken up in the morning. She'd opened the door to find someone at sentry waiting to watch over her as she'd prepared for the day.

At the sound of the metal panel clanging, she stood and opened the door to find Ancille with a smile on his face.

"Good morning. Are you ready to head out?"

She pushed her worries of Akin away and grinned. "Good morning. I'm ready."

In the Mess, she searched for Akin as she greeted the men who no longer stared at her as if she were a Miss Universe contestant during the swimsuit portion of the competition. The same quick glance proved Umale and Dubem missing from the room. She relaxed into her seat after getting her food.

She couldn't miss the excitement buzzing through the room. Maybe pirates had been found.

She ate a few bites. "What's going on?"

Ancille didn't need clarification to understand what she'd been referring to. "Helicopter delivery of supplies and mail."

That would do it. She caught the fervour even though she wouldn't be receiving anything. At least, their morale had risen. "That's good to hear."

Akin had taken her to their small commissary during her tour that first day. She'd been glad that her period had ended just before she'd come on board. Always prepared, she'd brought a sufficient supply of sanitary items with her. Relying on the ship's store would've left her in a lurch.

Whoever ran the naval system was serious about not having women aboard. After dealing with Umale and Dubem, she could understand why. How many other men on board the ship thought her to be some kind of whore to be passed around for their pleasure?

She shivered at the thought of pirates winning a battle against them. She'd be taken on board their ship and... She couldn't even think about the horrific things such ruthless people would do. Akin's dislike of her being on board wasn't as vicious as she'd initially thought.

She drank the last of her juice. "With everyone so happy, I doubt we'll have many people stopping by the sick bay today."

Ancille nodded. "I agree, but Commander Obatola has scheduled an emergency training."

Ishaq had to be the hardest working person she'd ever met. Operated on after a ruptured appendix and three days later back to work ordering them around, even if it was for half-day stretches. He'd ensure that they remained on their guard and prepared with emergency exercises.

She looked forward to whatever he had in store for them. "It should be an interesting day."

***

Akin dug his fingers into his shoulder in an attempt at massaging it while rotating his neck. He had refused to let the men's excitement of a delivery divert their attention from their training and work.

He stopped at Ishaq's cabin on the way back to his own. The one he shared with a woman he found harder and harder not to touch when he watched her at night once she'd fallen asleep. Her nightmare last night had given him the initiative to provide her comfort when she'd needed it most.

The fact that she'd yelled out Dubem's name before waking had disturbed him. It still did. Had something happened between them? Did she want it to? If she did, then why would the dream be a nightmare instead of something pleasant?

He flexed his fingers as he remembered the slightness of her hand in his, which had derailed him from the disturbing questions. For such a strong woman, she had small hands. Yet, they'd fitted in his so well that it had taken him longer than it should've to extract from her once she'd fallen asleep.

He rapped his knuckles against the door to a beat his friend would recognize.

"Come in," Ishaq called out. "Why do you even bother to knock?"

"I don't need to go blind walking in on you doing something I really would hate to see."

Ishaq's laughter came readily although he winced as he placed a hand on his abdomen. "I know it would mess you up to witness me painting my toenails."

Akin smiled and sat on the single bunk as he assessed his friend seated in the chair. "You're looking better."

"All thanks to Comfort."

He tried to tamp down the smile. He really did. "Yes. She did a good job."

"Everyone on the ship thinks you're sleeping together."

Always someone to speak his mind, the words didn't shock Akin. "We aren't."

Ishaq leaned forward with a slight grimace and looked him in the eyes. "You seem to like each other."

For once, Ishaq had managed to shock him.

"She can barely tolerate me. Besides—"

"Not from where I'm sitting every time you're in the same room. I've watched her with the men. Sure, she may be friendly with them, but she's honest and open with you."

Akin scoffed.

"You aren't making any sense." Bringing up Ishaq's wife should change the subject quick enough to put Akin at ease again. "Have you sent word to Georgina?"

"Comfort isn't afraid to be her real self with you." Ishaq refused to let the matter drop.

"Obstinate to the point of almost being disrespectful."

Ishaq rubbed a hand along his jaw. "Funny how she's not like that with anyone else. You seem to bring it out in her. And yet, she also makes you laugh."

Akin blinked at his friend.

"You don't do it often, so when someone catches it, you know the news will fly."

"So what? I laugh with you all the time."

Ishaq raised a brow.

Well, maybe he didn't. "It doesn't matter. My job is to keep her safe, not to have sex with her."

Not that the idea of them wrinkling the sheets together hadn't run through his mind and shot straight to his groin. A lot.

"She's good for you."

Akin stood and loomed over his friend. "We met a few days ago. How the hell can you tell that?"

Unfazed by the intimidation tactic, Ishaq rested his arm against his desk. "Dealing with people is what I do best. I know them. Remember?"

Akin marched to the door as his palms started to sweat. Ishaq could peg a person's personality from the first time he met them. Nine times out of ten, he'd be correct in his assessment.

"I just came by to check on you. Good to see you're doing better." He paused with his hand on the latch. "Do you need anything?"

"For retirement to arrive a few months early so I can go home and stay there."

Opposites when it came to the end of their careers, Akin would prefer to remain in the navy for the rest of his life. "How about something I can actually get you?"

Ishaq stood. "Be open to the possibility of you and Comfort being more than ... whatever the hell you are now."

It wasn't going to happen. He shook his head in response. "Goodnight."

As soon as they returned to Lagos, she'd be out of his life. His chest tightened at the thought. It didn't mean anything. He wouldn't let it.

CHAPTER SEVENTEEN

Tonight would be different. She'd get to the bottom of Akin's avoidance even if she had to tackle him to the floor to do it.

She really hoped it didn't come to that. Yes, her skills were impressive, but so were his. A test of who would win wasn't necessary. Especially since they were on the same team.

At least, Dubem had had the good sense to stay away from her. She'd have handled his manipulation with more force than she had yesterday.

Barre, the same person who'd escorted her the day before, had taken up the role for the evening. Several times on their way from the sick bay to her room, her stomach had churned as an eerie sense of being watched had encouraged her to turn. One of the many times she'd looked over her shoulder, she could've sworn she'd seen a shadow slip away.

She blamed the odd feeling on the video cameras strategically placed everywhere but the toilets, showers, and their cabins. Maybe Akin had told security to keep an extra watch on her since he refused to do it himself.

Akin snuck into the cabin just as he had the past three nights.

Before he could get undressed, she hopped out of her bunk and stood with her fists on her hips. Weary of shirking from this necessary confrontation, she went straight to the point. "Why have you been avoiding me?"

He faked an attempt to step forward to get to his rack. Unless he lifted her out of the way, she wasn't going anywhere.

"I'm tired. Move so I can get my things. "

By avoiding her question, had he just admitted what she'd merely speculated? Her stomach sank. Why should it hurt that he didn't want to be around her when she didn't care about him?

No. The truth rose to the surface. She *shouldn't* care about him.

"Not until you answer my question." She held up her index, middle, and ring finger. "It's been three days since we've spoken."

He cocked his head. "What does it matter? I've made sure you're safe. After that demonstration during training, I know you're more than capable of taking care of yourself. Hell, I fear for anyone who tries anything with you."

Warmth bloomed from her chest into every extremity at his unexpected praise. He may not do flowery words, but he knew how to compliment a woman.

She shoved her hand down as if deflecting his diversionary tactic. "Are you afraid of me?"

Every molecule in the room stilled at his sharp gaze. Blinking became impossible as he stepped into her space.

"Move." His voice came out as more of a deep-throated growl than a word.

Okay, so she was a teensy bit frightened. Not by the man, but how she'd pushed him to react. What had she been thinking asking such a question? Intimating that he feared anything? Wrong move.

Knees quivering, she held her ground. "Not until you tell me why you've been avoiding me."

Without warning, he had his hands under her arms. Braced to be rotated out of his way, she didn't expect his head to descend and crush her lips with his. Frozen, she took in the firmness of his mouth as his lips moved against hers. Her hands went to his shoulders to pull herself closer as she returned the kisses.

All sense of space and time fell away as his tongue entered her mouth and stroked hers. A moan escaped as she tilted her head, opening wider to him as she tasted the rich coffee flavour on his tongue. The scent of his soap had long ago faded, leaving a slight muskiness that had her breathing heavy. He smelled sexier than any man had the right to.

His hands stroking along her ribs and down her back ended up on her arse. She gasped as he lifted her, and she wound her legs around him. His strength added to her arousal as her back hit the cold metal of the top bunk. She'd never felt so alive in a man's arms. So desired.

He tore his mouth away from hers, and she gripped him harder when he nuzzled her neck, flicking his tongue to tease and then suck the sensitive skin. Not afraid of falling due to his considerable strength, she grasped the sides of his face, bringing his lips back to hers.

The kiss became even more passionate than the first as the juncture of her pyjama-clad thighs met the firmness of his abs. It wasn't enough as she rotated against him in an effort to get closer. Reaching down, she pulled at the base of his uniform top in an effort to get them skin to skin.

She had a hard time tugging it up. The realization that her legs wound around him acted as a sturdy belt penetrated her mind.

The existence of that reality brought others. What the hell were they doing? Yes, she'd dreamt of that moment, and it had exceeded her expectations, but...

But what?

Why couldn't she have him? Even on a temporary basis? Her life had been so hard. Why shouldn't she have him? Even if it was for just one night.

Her hesitation must've registered with Akin because he pulled away. Not only physically by releasing her so she slid the length of him to the floor, but she sensed an emotional withdrawal. A coldness seeped in where she'd been ablaze moments earlier.

Unable to maintain her own weight, she sank until her behind touched the bunk as he whirled away.

Their harsh breaths filled the air. Neither spoke. What could they say? They'd been about to... No. She would've stopped it before things had gotten too far.

Wouldn't she have?

His back remained to her.

"The crew thinks we're fu—" He stopped himself. "Involved."

He must've taken her silence to be shock and turned and pointed at her.

"You're a beautiful woman," he said in explanation regarding the men's presumptions. The fingertips of his large hands touched his chest. "I'm a male."

Brows scrunched together, she cocked her head and narrowed her eyes, trying to see what he hid. "There's got to be more to it. I know damn well they're aware that two people of the opposite sex can sleep in the same room without anything happening."

His deep inhale flexed his nostrils. "You made me laugh in front of them."

Opening her mouth to speak, she closed it with a popping sound and thought for a moment. "That makes no sense."

"I'm not one to laugh a lot. Because I did around you, they think we like each other. That's enough to justify their conjectures."

"But it's not true."

He bent and lifted his rack.

"It almost was tonight." He pulled out a T-shirt and shorts. "You asked why I've been staying away. I believe you got your answer."

She gripped her arms around herself, worried he wouldn't come back when he headed to the door. She held her ground instead of chasing after him. For once, her anxiety didn't stem from sleeping alone. Sleeping without him terrified her more.

A cold shower later, Akin entered the cabin. Comfort's curtain was closed. What had made him kiss her? One minute, she'd been stubborn as a goat, up in his face demanding an answer to a question he didn't want to answer. Her sweet scent wafting up to him. Enticing him.

Then the next, he'd sealed his fate when he'd laid his hands on her to lift her out of the way so he could get by.

The memory of her talented tongue swirling around his, the strength of her legs holding him prisoner as the passion flared between them, threatened to send him back for another shower. Only his hard-earned discipline kept him from opening the curtain to her sanctuary and tasting her again. Mint and pure Comfort. The headiest combination he'd ever experienced.

For both their sakes, they couldn't get involved. If it were possible, he'd send another soldier to sleep here with her. His gut burned at the thought. He didn't think she'd have sex with anyone else—at least, he hoped she wouldn't—but the bastard would have the pleasure of her company. Someone else would benefit from her laughter, strength, compassion, and intelligence. Everything that made her such an amazing woman.

He couldn't endure it.

He flipped over the blanket and lay on the bunk before covering his lower half. Just like he had the previous nights, he pretended to sleep and waited.

Time passed interminably slow before the light from her bunk created a red tint behind his lids.

Unlike the evenings before, she sighed before she got settled.

"What am I going to do with you?" her sweet voice whispered just loud enough for him to hear. "I can't have you, and yet, I want you so badly that I ache."

Akin forced himself to remain unmoving except for the controlled breaths which would help her to think she spoke to his unaware sleeping body.

When had things gotten complicated?

The moment I met her.

He'd known then that she was special. With her efficiency and unwillingness to back down from his most intimidating glares, she'd branded herself as different from the other women he'd known. He'd been immediately drawn to her, which had had him growling at Dubem to stay away from her.

And just like on that day, he also knew one thing. Even if she wanted something more than a fling, he had nothing to offer other than leaving her for the sea every chance he could get. She deserved better. A steady home. A man to shower her with love on a daily basis. To protect her. Sleep by her side every night. To be her anchor.

At the sound of her heavy, deep breaths, he opened his eyes and turned to face her. His heartbeats tripped over themselves. How could someone be so stunning? Inside and out.

He wasn't the man who'd provide her with what she needed in life.

Why not?

All he had to do was give up his career in order to gain a woman he'd never known he always wanted.

CHAPTER EIGHTEEN

Comfort's lungs burned as she pushed herself running on the treadmill in the ship's gym. Men had been waiting for it, but once they'd realized she also wanted to use it, they'd tripped over themselves to make sure she was next. Declining the offer hadn't worked, so she'd taken advantage of their kindness and tried not to be self-conscious about them watching her arse. She'd decided to ignore the hoot and whistle that had been blown her way.

Akin had woken her up early for PT. They'd walked to the training area with a distance between them. She couldn't figure out the major contributor of their unease. Although their newfound negative energy had caused her to walk as if she'd had a stick shoved into her spine, she had no will to change it. They needed to stay away from each other. For their own good.

She'd worked hard during the training in an attempt to burn off her frustration. It hadn't been enough, so she'd headed to the gym. When he'd insisted on staying with her, she'd been the one to purse her lips and narrow her eyes in warning.

"As you mentioned yesterday, they think we're sleeping together." Had he heard the desire in those last words? "Do you really think anyone would be idiotic enough to attempt to hurt me?"

Try to get her away from Akin and into their beds, yes. Hurt, she doubted.

He'd assigned one of the men to escort her back when she'd finished. She didn't argue because she'd probably have spent an hour trying to find her way if she'd gone back alone. She still couldn't understand how everyone wasn't walking around lost. Each passageway looked the same. Those directional signs Akin had finally relented to explain with much less patience than Ancille had had still just looked like numbers and letters with no meaning. She held out hope that she'd understand it one day.

She turned to the sailor who had delivered her to her cabin. "Thank you."

He tipped his head with a smile as he watched her go inside and close the door. Expecting an empty space, she jumped with a scream when she noticed Akin dressed in uniform sitting on the chair with a tablet in hand.

"Jeez. Aren't you supposed to be at work?"

He gestured to the device. "I'm working."

Stalking to her rack, she rolled her eyes. "I mean on the bridge, helm, weapons room, or wherever you disappear to during the day."

He chuckled, and the sound made her go still as a warm tingle tickled her scalp. Did he like her? Sure, they were attracted to each other, but liking someone was another beast all together. "What's so funny?"

"You make me sound like Batman hanging out in his lair."

Huh. The man kept surprising her. Another thing she had to fortify herself against. Gathering her things for the day, she turned towards the door. Not surprised when he stood to follow, she didn't try to stop him. One fight per morning was enough. Besides, she'd won it, as evidenced by his not hovering in the gym. Might as well stay ahead.

She'd gotten into a routine when it came to showering. Organization was the name of the game when sharing facilities. Today, knowing that Akin stood outside waiting for her after what they'd shared last night, routine went out the window. She turned the handle to cold. Never had she showered so quickly.

Rubbing her skin with her favourite lotion to bring back the circulation the frigid water had stolen, she still couldn't get her teeth to stop chattering. No more ridiculous cold showers for her.

Then cease and desist with the erotic thoughts about Akin.

She stepped out of the shower area dressed in an oversized navy uniform that matched Ancille's and Ishaq's. The sight of Akin's broad shoulders and how he'd been able to lift her without any effort had her catching her breath.

She breezed past him and into the room, put her things away, and made her bed before turning to him. "I'm ready."

For more than just work. If she didn't control her hormones, she'd end up lost and alone. With the memories of the way his mouth had sucked on her bottom lip, she could almost guarantee he'd ensure a satiating sexual experience if she gave in. She wouldn't.

On the way to the Mess, her curiosity got the best of her. "What made you join the navy?"

From the slight smirk he flashed at her, she knew she'd opened a whole jar of personal rather than keeping it closed like she should've.

Now, he knew. She liked him.

It had only taken one question to dissipate the tension smothering him. The uneasiness had clawed onto his back and wouldn't let go. Until that moment.

"It's a long story."

She bowed her head, confirming that with her question, she'd desired to be let into his life somehow. To know a little more about him.

"Okay."

Rubbing a hand over his freshly shaved chin, he considered her response. No fight? She'd really wanted to know more about him. He probably shouldn't be forcing himself to hold back a grin because of the sudden happiness at her misery.

"How about instead of you playing poker with the guys tonight, we hang out on the deck and I'll tell you my story."

Wide eyes met his, and her smile made his belly heat.

"How did you know?"

"There are very few secrets on this ship. These men gossip like retired old women. I also have spies who let me know where you are."

They'd reached the Mess when she glared at those eating. "They're *all* spies."

He maintained a neutral expression.

"Yes." He shrugged. "Your safety is a priority."

"Huh." She grunted. "If I catch them at it, they'll feel my wrath."

She winked as she turned her back on him.

This time, he bit down hard on his cheek to stop the guffaw of laughter wanting to escape. She knew how to soften the hardness within him. She also possessed the keen ability to anger him with one of her defiant squints.

Why now? How come she'd entered his life only to disturb it? To make him question the rock-solid decision to stay in the navy instead of retiring?

***

Akin and Comfort hadn't spoken since his brusque greeting when he'd escorted her to the Mess after work. Not a word during the meal. And yet, giddiness threatened to make Comfort giggle for no damn reason when they reached the deck.

What was it about Akin that being with him made her feel alive? He was a man, nothing more or less. A big, brutish one who commanded with fierce determination and knew how to push her buttons. Yet, he'd also shown an empathetic and gentle side. At least towards her—she doubted his sailors ever saw that aspect of him.

She tipped her head back and attempted to take everything in. "There are so many stars in the sky."

He caught her by the shoulders when she stumbled. The warmth from his large hands didn't linger long enough before he pulled them away.

"This is far enough. Don't get close to the rail," his deep voice said near her ear, sending tingles down her neck.

"We don't want to lose you to the sea. The presence of no lights other than from us means we can see more stars."

Glimmering stars overtook the midnight blue dome she normally only noticed when she made an effort to observe the night sky. This was different. Even the moon had its own gloriousness. She'd never seen anything more stunning in her life.

She blinked back the burn of tears as she angled her shoulders to look up at him.

Bending his knees, he came closer to eye level with downcast brows and a deep groove between his eyes. "What's wrong, Princess?"

Her stomach flipped. She loved when he called her Princess. She didn't feel like one, but he made it sound as if she actually was.

She swiped the back of her hand at the moisture which had escaped. "It's so beautiful."

Rising to his full height, he nodded. "It certainly is. The combined vastness of the sea and sky makes you realize how insignificant we are."

She stared upward. This time, she backed into his chest and leaned on the strength he provided. His warmth seeped into her, and she never wanted to leave the sanctuary of his body. When had she ever felt this safe? This connected? They stayed glued together even when a guard patrolled past.

Honesty flowed from her.

"I never understood why I was spared from death. I don't think I ever will." She wrapped her arms around herself, wishing he'd do it for her. But he stood with his hands at his sides. "My family was amazing. Everyone had these special gifts, and they knew just how to use them to help people."

She watched the course of a falling star. She'd learned a long time ago about the futility of making wishes. "I'm plain compared to them. Not the best at anything. I'm not special."

His voice vibrated at her back. "You are."

How would he know? He didn't.

"No. I'm not. If you'd met my family, you'd understand." She reached up to see if she could touch the majestic jewels in the sky. Of course she couldn't. "They were the most charismatic people you could ever meet. They didn't even have to speak. Just being in their presence, you knew they were destined for greatness. But they only made it to the point that they did, and I'm stuck here to live without their light."

Strong arms wrapped around her, stealing away the chill which had permeated into her bones.

"I don't understand how you can't see how exceptional you are," he whispered in her ear.

"If you had known them—"

He spun her around, keeping his hands on her upper arms.

"I know *you*. I've experienced your glowing personality and have had the chance to be touched by it." He shook his head. "I don't know why you were left behind. But I'm not sorry you were. You have so much to offer the world. Your work is not done. Deep down, you know it. Otherwise, you wouldn't have been the strong woman standing before me today."

Soft lips pressed against her forehead, and the dam of tears broke like it hadn't in years.

"Let it out, Princess. I'm here for you."

Akin rocked her and rubbed her back while she wept into his chest.

She'd been alone for so long. Roaming from one life-altering devastation with MSF to another in an attempt to hide from her own pain. From the destruction which had become her life.

As she clung to Akin, the sobs shook her body. Agonizing pain made her abs contract. Yet, it was better than holding them in like she'd done over the years. She'd

had to be there for those whose lives had been torn apart.
No time for self-pity. Who would've cared?

Tears flowed for her family and the people her medical
skills hadn't been able to save.

For the first time, with the support of someone she
barely knew but trusted with her life, she cried for herself.

CHAPTER NINETEEN

Akin walked Comfort to the outside wall of the helicopter hangar and sat her down in a shadowed area when the heaving sobs began to abate. When he'd tucked her into his side, nothing could've slipped between them. He never wanted to release her. He refused to let the world intrude on them and sink her back into the negativity and guilt she'd wallowed in for years. The debilitating solitude.

She clung to him. Could she feel how hard his heart beat under her hand?

"I'm sorry." Her voice came out raspy.

"For what?"

"Crying all over you."

He flexed his arm, pulling her closer. "I would've expected an apology if you hadn't. It's been coming since that day you told me your story, hasn't it?"

"Probably longer. Ever since my ex-husband left me, I don't cry for myself anymore. He told me I wasn't the woman he'd married. I interpreted his words to mean that I'd become weak. My family had been my strength, and without them..."

Loosening his hold, he pulled himself back to hook a finger under her chin so she could look him in the eyes. She needed to see the truth of his words.

"No, Comfort. You're strong. You always have been, and I don't doubt you always will be. Your ex was the weak one for expecting you to heal from such grave heartbreak without changing. For not being able to remember that everything passes. Everything. And not sticking by you until it did."

Warm air fanned his cheek when she expelled a shuddering breath.

"He had every right. Hell, I'm surprised he stayed as long as he did. We hadn't been getting along for the year prior. We were both overworked and…"

"What?" He prodded with a jiggle of her shoulder.

"I had been putting off having a baby for a while." She lowered her gaze. "I wasn't ready to lose the foothold I'd gotten on my career. If we'd had a child, he would've proceeded while I'd been held back. I wasn't ready to make the sacrifice." She focused on him again. "I guess that makes me selfish."

Akin smiled. "Only as selfish as anyone else, male or female, who wants to make a career for themselves. It's just that women are expected to fall back, at least for a while, when they have a child while men continue forward."

Her brows bunched together. "If I didn't know better, I'd think you were a feminist."

Free from witnesses, he released the laughter. How did she have the uncanny ability to set him free? "What makes you think I'm not?"

She pointed a finger towards the sky. "You're mean to women."

"I'm mean to everyone."

"True." A second digit flipped up. "You don't want female sailors on your ship."

He grabbed her hand and laced their fingers together. How could such a small structure fit so perfectly into his?

"It's not my rule. We're on a pirate-seeking ship where there's a risk of being attacked. Pirates have no honour. I'd hate to think what would happen to a woman if she were ever captured during a siege."

An icy chill stole down his spine at the thought of it ever happening with Comfort on board.

"I've been thinking about it while here, and you're right. I honestly don't think I would've taken the mission if I'd known I was the only female on board."

He hadn't wanted her on the ship, but was immensely glad she'd joined him. A feeling of wholeness filled his chest where he hadn't noticed the emptiness before. His world would have continued spinning, but not with as much vigour if she hadn't stepped onto *Reckoning*. It was easier to deal with facts than emotion.

"I have no qualms about working with female sailors. I can name several I would've been honoured to have on this ship if the risks weren't so great for them."

Her mouth dropped open, bringing his focus directly to her lips. Remembering how soft they'd been under his. How pliant. She'd made him forget everything except the pleasure of her kisses and her body. His groin stirred.

Yanking his attention away from temptation, he looked out at the sky and sucked in the cool sea air. Time to divert his mind to something less volatile. "What's your third point?"

"I'm too stumped about the second one to come up with a third. Hell, I give up. Commander Akin Solarin is a feminist."

"If you ever tell anyone, I'll lock you in the brig and feed you boiled carrots."

Her laughter warmed him, and he desired nothing more at that moment than to hear more of it.

She raised her left hand while the right landed on her chest. "I promise. Only because no one would believe me."

They sat in silence for a while.

Akin stood at the sound of the guard's footfalls. "Let's get you something to drink."

"How do you know I'm thirsty?"

Rather than pointing to the damp stain on his uniform demonstrating how much liquid she'd lost in the form of tears, he shook his head. "You're so damn stubborn. Fine, let's get *me* something to drink."

She placed a hand on his cheek. "I don't care what people say about you or what you show the world. You're a sweet man. Thank you for being so kind to me."

His chest tightened at the sincerity in her tone. "Any time."

And he meant it. He'd show her his heart if that's what she needed to make her life easier. To boost her morale and make sure she always remembered just how much strength she possessed.

They walked together to the closest water fountain on the deck below. As he watched her attempt to drain the water supply, he realized just how much he cared about her. In an impossibly short time, she'd made him feel something other than the need to be the best in his career. Not that it would help either of them. They were destined for different things. And none of them included being together.

Comfort had never experienced such an emotional catharsis. Her eyes were puffy and probably red enough to scare the devil himself, but she didn't care. Akin had seen her at her worst and stayed when he could've dropped her off in her room and run in the opposite direction. He'd held her close and encouraged her to release her misery.

His words had hit home. She'd carried the burden of survivor's guilt for so long. Too damn long. Not completely free, at least now, she could see there was a light somewhere in her future. One which Akin had helped to point her towards. She'd forever be grateful.

After grabbing some water, she'd insisted they return to the deck. How could she give up the spectacular view of the starlit sky which had helped to free her?

"What made you join the navy?"

After the drama they'd experienced, had he thought she'd forgotten what had brought them there earlier in the evening?

"Poverty."

She waited for him to continue. The moments ticked by as waves skimmed the ocean's surface and lapped against the side of the ship.

"That can't be the story. A beginning, middle, and an end would be nice."

"I'm the second to last of eight children. By the time my mother had me, she'd been barely able to feed the six before me. Much less herself, but she was determined to keep her creations alive, so she farmed until her palms were more calloused than smooth." He rubbed his hands together. "She turned us all into farmers. She always found a way to make sure we ate and had what we needed. She taught me the meaning of strength."

"Where was your father?"

He stroked his broad jaw and grunted. "Let's just say he only came home to make sure my mother got pregnant. He was successful one more time after me."

Incredulity held her frozen. "Leaving your mother with eight children to raise on her own?"

"Until she died when I was twelve."

She placed a hand on his upper arm. "You have my condolences."

He looked into her eyes. "Thank you. Her life was more difficult than anyone's should've been. And yet, she'd kept on surviving. Trying to give us the best of what she could afford. She put all of us in school. Our uniforms were used and torn, and we had no shoes, notebooks, or anything else the teachers told us to bring, but we were always on time. Back then, education was free, and they fed us. It was a meal she didn't have to worry about. We got embarrassed when others made fun of us. When we complained to my mother, she'd listen, nod, and then tell us that no matter what anyone said or did, we should always do."

He smiled.

"Not even try, but do." He diverted his attention back to the sea. "She was a remarkable woman."

"I can imagine."

Guilt bit into her. She'd seen it on her missions with MSF. Sometimes parents, especially the women, were willing to give up every comfort in their lives for their children. Hell, she hadn't even been willing to temporarily slow down her career to even try to have a child. Would she have been willing to give everything up for them?

The tension in her shoulders diminished as the answer rushed into her. *Yes.* If she'd had a child, she would've done anything to ensure his or her prosperity.

"The oldest four children left for the city and found jobs. They sent money whenever they could, easing our mother's burden."

He went quiet for a moment. "We returned from school one day to find the house quiet instead of filled with her singing. Her favourite were songs that gave thanks to her maker. She'd tell us that the best way to live was to be grateful and treat everyone well. No matter what."

Did she really want to hear the rest? Whether she did or not, she would. It was the least she could do. She slipped her hand into his, attempting to infuse him with the strength he claimed she possessed. Did he feel the same tingles skittering up his arm like she did?

Looking straight ahead, he adjusted them so their fingers linked.

"I went through our small hut and into the sleeping area. She lay on her back with the sweetest smile on her face. For the first time in my life, she looked like she'd found peace. We were devastated to lose her. We couldn't have had a better person to call our mother."

He bumped against her shoulder with his. "In some ways, you remind me of her. Practical, strong, enduring, hardworking, and kind."

Her heart performed an unexpected summersault. Delighted to be compared to the one woman he'd probably respected most in his life, she smiled in acceptance of the best compliment she'd ever received.

CHAPTER TWENTY

How long had it been since he'd told the story of his childhood? Akin couldn't remember his ex-wife being interested enough to ask about what had driven him into the navy.

Comfort had listened as if she'd wanted to learn every detail. As if she cared about the lady who'd sacrificed her life to help her children achieve what she hadn't. Akin loved the woman who'd raised him to be the man he'd become. Her teachings and influence would remain with him until he joined her one day.

The female at his side squeezed their enjoined hands. Her warmth infusing into him brought a sense of harmony he couldn't ever remember feeling.

"What happened next?" her soft voice asked.

"After the burial, my eldest brother took us to the city with him." He smiled. "I had never seen so many people gathered together before. So much was happening that I refused to sleep just in case I missed something."

"Sounds like a Johnny-just-come to me."

He nodded. "Exactly. My neck got the workout of its life as I tried to take everything in. My brother found me a job as a house help. To make a long story short, I worked hard for them, just like my mother had taught me to do. I was there for two months before her husband came home. I had to arch my back to look up at his face. And his uniform had me mesmerized."

He laughed at the memory of how he'd behaved that day. Gawking and stumbling over his words. "I'm sure he thought I could neither hear, talk, nor possessed the ability to close my mouth. I was just so in awe of him. I'd never come into contact with a man who emitted such dignity and power. When I got over my wonderment and was able to answer his questions, I told him I could read and write when he'd asked. He decided to send me to school."

Comfort gasped at the man's generosity.

He'd been lucky to find such a home to work in. "Not the private one his own children attended, but I wasn't bothered by that. I went to school and made sure to do the work I was given in the house and more. The family was pleased with me. When I graduated senior high school, he asked if I wanted to join the navy."

The elation which had filled him that day bubbled up in his chest. "He didn't have to ask me twice. He got me in, and here I am."

"He must be proud of what you've accomplished."

Akin thought about the man he considered to be more of a father than his own had ever been. "He is. We still keep in touch. I see them a couple times a year."

She pursed her lips to the side. "What about your brothers and sisters?"

"My mother taught us that family is everything. We're still close." He winked. "You'd be surprised to learn that I'm not the most aggressive one of my siblings."

"Who does the honour go to?"

"My eldest sister." He shook his upper body in a fake shiver. "She definitely knows how to get her way. My ex-wife was afraid of her."

Comfort looked at him with wide eyes. "You were married?"

He'd experienced the same sort of shock when she'd spoken about her ex. "Yes."

She pulled her hand from his and crossed her arms over her chest. They sat in silence as the multitude of stars bore witness.

Would she ask about his failed marriage? He didn't wait for the questions to come.

"I'm sure you've heard about the reputation of the navy. A woman at each port and things like that."

"Did you cheat on her?"

"Not once. I was referring to my younger years. It turns out that charm isn't a prerequisite for getting a woman when you're in the military. The uniform is all that they need. The fact that money is flowing helps, too. After about eight years in the navy, I met my now ex-wife. When she got pregnant, I did the right thing and married her after just three months of knowing her. She lost the baby a week after the ceremony."

How many times had he wondered if she'd ever been pregnant to begin with? He'd taken her word for it.

"I'm sorry for your loss," Comfort said with a gentle tone.

"Thank you. After a while, she became annoyed with the time I spent away from her. She blamed me for her not getting pregnant again because I was never around at the right time, and she started dropping hints that I quit the navy. She eventually became less subtle and demanded it. I spent my time at home fighting with her. It wasn't a pleasant situation."

"Did you ever consider leaving the navy for her?"

The hairs at the back of his neck stood on edge with the anxiety he heard in the question.

"I fell in love with the navy long before I joined it. The first moment I saw my boss towering above me in his uniform, I knew I wanted to be just like him. I excelled in basic training. I had someone I had to prove myself to. Someone I wanted to be proud of me. When I first set foot on a ship, I became lost to the sea." He rubbed a fist over his sternum, remembering the joy and wonder which had possessed him. "Nothing had ever felt so right."

Every decision he'd made over the years had led him to finding Comfort. He turned and gazed at her. A similar feeling of rightness shifted in his chest. Who was she to him? How had she come to be in his life when it had been moving along smoothly without complications?

She caught him staring. "So you're in the navy until they kick you out?"

For the first time, he couldn't give a positive answer. "Unless I'm motivated to do otherwise. What about you? Have you ever thought about settling down somewhere?"

Where had that question come from? It didn't matter—his palms sweated with the need to hear the answer.

She shrugged. "I've been running so fast and hard from my demons that I haven't had time to think about it. Working with MSF is rewarding."

"Do you want a family?" He squelched the urge to clamp his hand over his mouth at the invasiveness of his query. "Never mind. It's none of my business."

She sighed. "I think I do. I believe that with my experiences, I've outgrown my selfishness. I'm willing and ready to make others a priority in my life."

His heart thumped faster. Why was he so excited about her being willing to settle down? It shouldn't matter one way or another. Once they finished this tour, they'd drop her off, and she'd be out of his life. Forever.

His jaw clenched as he ground his teeth. The thought didn't sit right.

She shifted back and held up both hands. "What the hell has you so angry?"

Pretending to yawn made it turn into a real one. He looked at his watch to see that it was past one in the morning.

"I'm tired," he lied. He could sit talking with her for the rest of the night and never miss the lack of sleep.

She studied him for a moment before getting to her feet. "Time to hit the sack. I wouldn't want to make the men suffer by stealing away your much-needed rest."

He couldn't count how many times she'd made him laugh this evening. What was one more? He stood. "If they don't do their jobs well, they'll feel my wrath regardless of my mood."

"Good point."

The walk to the cabin didn't take long. Both of them too exhausted to shower, he gave her privacy by waiting outside while she changed into her night clothes. When she opened the door, he stepped in. Even fully covered in her pale blue pyjama bottoms and a matching T-shirt, she enticed him. She slid into her bunk and closed the curtains.

"Good night, Akin."

"Good night."

Had she released enough of her tormented past tonight to be able to sleep without him in the room anymore? He'd be happy for her if she had. At the same time, he didn't want to give up sleeping across from her. If only he could have her in his arms, clinging to him as he slid into her until she moaned with her release.

He snuffed out the fantasy. As much as he desired her, he was her protector. Other than the incredible kiss they'd shared, he'd make sure nothing more happened between them. They were on the ship to do their jobs, and he'd make sure they did. No matter how difficult he found it to keep his hands off her captivating body.

CHAPTER TWENTY-ONE

Comfort had woken up with the curtain to her bunk closed. Confused, she rolled onto her back. The last thing she remembered was waiting to hear Akin's familiar, deep breathing as her signal to draw open the material and watch him sleep. Every night, she'd undertaken the same ritual. The slow rise and fall of his muscular chest had gotten her to sleep faster than any sleeping pill her psychiatrist had recommended.

She must've fallen asleep on her own. Perhaps she'd just been bone-tired. A quick look at her watch revealed the time to be six a.m. Akin must've gone.

With a sigh, she slid open her curtain and swung her feet off the bed, careful not to bang her head against the top bunk when she lifted her torso. Feet planted on the floor, she rested her elbows on her knees and rubbed her eyes. Swollen and gritty. Crying sucked.

Although the heaviness which had weighed her down since her family's death had lightened. She smiled at a memory of them surrounding her in bed and scaring the hell out of her by screaming for her to wake up on her sixteenth birthday. For the first time, she let other pleasant thoughts of them filter in without stopping them. She'd had the best family she could've ever asked for.

Damn, she missed them. What wouldn't she give to have more time with them? To laugh with them again. To have another conversation with each of them. No matter what she offered up as a sacrifice, it wouldn't be enough. She'd have to wait until her time came to be with them again. She swallowed hard and knew for the first time since the accident that she could wait.

As Akin had mentioned last night, she'd been spared for a reason. God didn't make mistakes. She now accepted it.

"What has you smiling so early in the morning?"

She bolted upright with a yelp and hit her head at the sound of the deep familiar voice.

"Ouch." She sucked in air through her teeth as she rubbed the injured area. Now she knew why so many people came to the sick bay with head injuries. "What the hell are you doing here?"

The man had difficulty speaking as he rolled onto his side with laughter.

She should be annoyed. How could she be when the joyous sound tickled her more than wiggly fingers against her feet? All she could do was watch him with a smile plastered across her face as her stomach flipped. His light skin glowed with a pink hue, and his chocolate brown eyes shone.

He finally got himself under control.

"I'm sorry." He sucked in a breath before letting out a few more chuckles. "Are you okay?"

She wiped the grin from her face and did her best impression of his scowl. "I'm fine. No thanks to you. What are you doing here?"

"Last I checked, it's my cabin."

She rolled her eyes and got to her feet. "I mean, why are you still here? You're usually gone by this time."

Akin swung his legs off the side of the bed, stood, and stretched. His shirt hitched up, revealing the skin she'd so desperately wanted to touch the other day when her legs had been wrapped around him. He'd left her in a state of longing with those hot kisses.

Face flushed, she looked up to find that his eyes had darkened as he watched her. She cleared her throat. "Um, we have to get ready."

He gave her a sharp nod and turned to lift his rack. Following his example, she did the same and tried to focus on pulling out clothes for the day rather than on the throbbing between her thighs.

With her things in hand, she placed them on the top bunk before bending over to make her bed. A low groan from behind made her glance over her shoulder. Akin had his gaze glued to her rear. Her heart thudded as every part of her body became hot. She had half a mind to back up and shift to the left until she made contact with that vital part of him.

Where had the need to stay as far away from him disappeared to? Desire she wanted to drown in had replaced it. What did it matter if they didn't end up together? At least, she would've experienced being with him instead of hiding. The old her had never run or hidden from anything or anyone. Her body hummed with her return to being who she'd always known herself to be.

Standing upright, she rotated on her heel to face him.

He hitched a thumb towards the door. "I'll be in the shower."

The moment had passed.

"I'll be there in a minute."

Her skin tingled at the thought of joining him in his. She cleared her head with a nod and then waited for him to leave before slumping onto her bed. She'd been a second away from seducing him.

She filled her lungs to help eradicate the regret at a lost opportunity. It would've been so easy. His eyes spoke of passion. Now that she was ready to live fully, she'd take advantage of the opportunity to be with him the next time it came around. She'd make sure he understood what she needed from him so that his ethical ways wouldn't reject her out of fear of taking advantage of her.

Deep down, they both knew better. Their attraction had sparked the day they'd met. At the right time, she'd make sure Akin knew how much she wanted him and that she expected nothing from him but his body.

Was that all she needed? Her heart said no, but it would be all she'd get.

***

Akin should've been dead on his feet after a long morning of preparedness training with his men. Two hours of sleep shouldn't have him feeling as if he could run a ten-kilometre race. He'd waited for Comfort to open her curtain last night, but she never had. She hadn't tossed or turned, either, and after twenty minutes, he'd peeked inside to find her knocked out.

Sitting in the empty conference room waiting for the executive team to arrive for the emergency meeting the captain had called, he smiled. Comfort had made progress.

Laughter was accompanied by a strong hand pounding his shoulder.

"What evil plot of physical training has you grinning? Or is it our lovely doctor that has this softening effect on you?"

Akin wiped all traces of amusement from his face and glared at Dubem. He still hadn't forgiven his XO for the several times he'd flirted with Comfort. Jealousy over the man's natural charm hadn't sat right with him, especially since he considered Dubem a good friend.

Dubem chuckled again. "If only women knew how much power they truly have over us."

The statement definitely applied to him. Comfort had him by the ear.

Sitting in his usual seat, Dubem strummed his fingers against the table.

"Umale told me that he'd tried for a chance at her and she'd rejected him." Dubem's eyes narrowed, and a slight snarl marred his normally jovial face. "Looks like she thinks she's too good for some of us."

Akin's good humour from moments ago disappeared. Why had Dubem's demeanour changed so drastically? As if he'd been the one shunned instead of Umale.

He shook his head and tamped down the need to beat the boy. Why hadn't Comfort told him? "That hothead would've never stood a chance with her. He's barely able to use the minimum common sense God gave him."

When Umale had come on board at Dubem's request, Akin had been against it.

While serving on another ship years ago, Akin had written an honest evaluation that the boy had issues with respecting authority and was not an effective worker. Umale's animosity had been thrown towards Akin ever since he'd learned that his denial of promotion from Mid-Shipman to Acting Sub-Lieutenant was in part due to Akin. As long as the boy never disrespected him to his face, they'd have no issues. It had taken Umale an extra three years to be promoted.

At the time, he hadn't been able to understand how Umale had become an officer in the first place. Years later, he'd discovered the familial relationship with Dubem. Dubem had taken his nephew in when his eldest sister had died. She'd never stated who the father of the baby had been. If only Dubem could teach Umale how to be a better person, things would go well for him, both in and out of the navy.

Dubem shrugged.

"No one likes to be rejected." His laughter sounded hollow. "As conservative as she seems to be, she must be a wildcat in bed for you to be grinning like you were. The freaks are always quiet. Anytime you're ready to share more than stories, brother, I'm here."

Rage hit him like an anvil dropped on a nail. The other commanding officers, including Ishaq, trooped into the room before he could drive Dubem to the wall with his forearm at his throat.

Rather than make a violent scene at the blatant disrespect of the woman who'd come on board to help them, he looked Dubem in the eyes.

"If you ever talk about her like that again, you won't ever have to worry about impressing people with your smile because you won't have any teeth." The threat in his voice had the two commanders who'd just entered looking between them. "Are we clear, *brother*?"

Dubem wouldn't be able to take Akin on in a fight, and he knew it. He raised his hands and grinned. "I was just joking, man. Take it easy."

"I hope a woman isn't getting between you," Lewis said. "They really aren't worth it. They'll open their legs for anyone. It's the selfishness of their nature. Best not to get attached."

The man's negative attitude towards women whenever they conversed had always annoyed Akin. He'd never learned why, but the guy seemed to hate them.

Before Akin could leap over Gowon and slam Lewis' head into the table, the captain arrived. They all stood.

Akin attempted to control his temper so he could focus on the emergency meeting. The mission mattered more than anything else.

"We have a situation." The man dove in with no preamble.

Akin clenched his jaw as trepidation slammed into him. Not for him or his men, but for Comfort. Tomorrow, they'd reach Lagos, and she'd be safe on shore. It would be best for any issues to happen after they'd dropped her off.

"Sensors have detected two ships at fifty miles starboard. When we communicated asking them to identify themselves, we received no response from either ship."

The tension in the room elevated as everyone sat straighter.

"Pirate jacking?" someone asked.

"From what we can surmise, I'm suspecting it to be. We're getting closer to assess. I need you all prepared for battle."

Adrenalin-infused blood hammered through Akin. The sailors under his jurisdiction were always ready.

They talked strategy for rest of the short meeting before the captain discharged them to their duties. They left to organize for what no one hoped would turn into a violent situation. If it did, they'd be the victors.

Dubem stopped him in the passageway. "I was just joking before. Are we cool?"

A punch to the man's perfect face would make things better. Since they had a situation to contend with, he nodded his consent before walking away.

Moments later, the captain made an announcement over the loudspeaker. The ship became a buzz of activity. Even those on off duty and resting joined the impending fray. Everyone had a role during times of battle. The drills they'd grumbled through would serve them well. His men knew how to handle themselves.

His concern for Comfort had him more anxious than anything else. He made his way to the sick bay wondering if he'd have to convince her to stay in her work area. Safe.

He nodded in approval at their established emergency readiness, which included having the medications and supplies they'd need easily at hand.

"Comfort." He levelled her with his most intense stare. "You're to stay here."

Her nose flared at the order. Would she argue?

She gave a brisk nod as her army training seemed to emerge.

Pride tightened his throat. Damn, he wished he could kiss her. Why hadn't he done so last night when they'd obviously both wanted it? What the hell was the point of life but to live it?

He wouldn't make that mistake again. He'd ensure they got the opportunity once everything settled.

Akin went to Ishaq and placed a hand on his shoulder. He looked better than he had days ago when they'd rushed him off the ship to the hospital. Words weren't necessary as Ishaq nodded. As he would for any of his comrades, his friend would protect Comfort with his life.

He turned and left the sick bay only to be stopped by Comfort's hand against his arm.

When he turned, she saluted. "Give 'em hell, Commander."

He returned the salute, and not giving a damn who saw, bent his head and kissed her hard on the lips.

"Stay safe, Princess."

Then, he pivoted and left the woman who'd burrowed her way into his heart.

CHAPTER TWENTY-TWO

Comfort bounced in her seat as they gathered in the Mess. Akin hadn't shown up yet.

Why did she miss him so much? She knew he was safe. Yet, the jittery feeling inside her wouldn't settle until she'd lain eyes on him.

During the heightened alarm stage, she and the other medics had waited in the sick bay ready to treat any condition that was brought in. Her nerves had been stretched taut the whole time as she'd prayed like she'd never done before.

God must've decided to listen to her because everyone on board had survived without injury. She couldn't say the same for the pirates' bodies, which had been loaded onto their ship and transported to the shore.

The transfer of the ship and bodies to the authorities on land had taken much longer than their violent encounter had.

The story had been retold many times directly from the weapons specialists who'd been at the scene. The retrieval crew had told an even grimmer tale of the bullet-riddled bodies. The marauders had attacked a Liberian ship carrying cocoa. When they'd realized that the navy destroyer had decided to apprehend them, they'd taken off in a motorboat.

The foolish pirates had fired on the ship in their attempt to escape. Their shots had fallen way short of their mark. The bullets from the *Reckoning* hadn't missed. The pirates had decided to continue firing, so the captain had had no choice but to end the squirmish by filling the boat and the pirates with bullets. Calling it a battle would've be an exaggeration. Massacre was more the word she'd use.

The crew of the ship the pirates had attempted to plunder were shaken, but no one had been injured. It may not have been the case if they hadn't intervened.

As a healer, the loss of life, even the enemy's, had upset her. She couldn't fathom the psychology behind their behaviour. By firing at *Reckoning*, they'd basically committed suicide.

"Why didn't the pirates give in?" she asked. "Wave a white flag? Radio their surrender? Anything to ensure their survival."

"They have no honour!" one of the men shouted. The others in the Mess roared.

"They knew that if we captured them," Ishaq said in a calmer manner, "we'd get information that they aren't ready to give."

She scrunched her brows together. "So they'd rather die?"

"They live by a code." Ishaq's fierce snarl was accompanied by a head shake. "As warped as it is. Bringing them on board means we could extract information from them about their comrade pirates and financial sponsors. If we can cut off the cash flow, we can stop the piracy. Even if they give us nothing useful, once they're seen stepping off our ship, their lives would've been snuffed out by their own. They chose to go down fighting."

Her jaw hurt as she ground her teeth together. "And still lost."

Ishaq shrugged. "It's the life they know and choose to live and die by. Preferring to appease their greed over anything else, including survival. I'd be surprised if they had anyone in their lives they hadn't betrayed at one point or another. They'd prefer to live by the—"

"Gun and die by the gun." Comfort jumped in with an adaptation of the old adage.

"Exactly."

For the next ten minutes, the discussion revolved around piracy and how much damage it caused. After a while, the conversation became lighter, and jokes flew. Pain from uncontrollable laughter had settled into Comfort's ribs by the time she decided to end her time with the guys.

Ishaq stood when she did. "I'll walk you."

She glanced across the room at Dubem. The bastard had the audacity to wink. Her face flushed with anger. Balling her fist, she wanted to punch him in the offending eye. She'd enjoyed Umale's absence.

Akin was another matter as she watched the entrance hoping he'd show up. "Where's the bear?"

"I don't know. I haven't seen him since the debriefing when he returned from delivering the pirate ship to the authorities on shore. He normally joins us after an altercation. It's a good way for everyone to decompress."

"It sure is. I haven't laughed so hard in years."

Ishaq chuckled. "Make sure you explain to Akin that the glassiness of your eyes is from the after-effects of joy. Otherwise, there'll be more battles. This time on the ship."

Her insides warmed. She bowed her head to hide her pleasure at how much of an interest Akin had taken in her. "He's a little overprotective."

Ishaq snorted. "A little? I'd rather deal with a lioness guarding her cubs than him protecting you. If anything had happened to you today, let's just say my wife wouldn't have been able to recognize me when I got home."

She rolled her eyes and sucked her teeth. "You're being dramatic."

Her colleague raised a brow. "Am I?"

No. Ishaq had a tendency of saying what he meant.

He tipped his head in a mock bow when they reached her cabin. "I'll see you tomorrow."

"Our last day."

"Yes. We'll be pulling into port at Lagos in the afternoon. That's unless anything happens between here and there." His eyes glazed over as he smiled. "I'm looking forward to being with my family. Not that I didn't appreciate them before, but feeling the breath of death directly against my cheek has given life a whole new perspective."

In her case, she hadn't wanted to live. Now, she couldn't imagine not being in the world.

"Yeah." Her voice held empathy. "Goodnight."

The adrenalin had burned off, and now, a sense of gloom threatened to suffocate her. In less than twenty-four hours, she wouldn't see Akin again. He'd given her so much. As stern and gruff as he presented himself, he possessed a gentle spirit. She'd miss him. More than she had a right to after knowing him for only a week.

Comfort stalled when she walked in to find Akin standing on the other side of the cabin.

He closed the space between them in a blur of movement. Before she could fathom his intention, his rough hands were framing her face as he studied her.

"What's wrong? Why have you been crying?"

Her limbs went limp at the intensity of his concern. Reaching up, she clasped onto his forearms. His tantalizing heat seeped into her. "I was laughing with the guys in the Mess. How come you didn't join us?"

He lowered his head. When their lips touched, the familiar current flowed into her. His gentle kisses glazed over her lips like syrup, sweet and addictive, making her cling to him for support.

"If I had gotten anywhere near you, I would've snatched you away and brought you to the room to make love."

Her legs wobbled.

He pressed a kiss to her cheek and rubbed his nose against the same spot. "I didn't need them seeing how much of a weakness you are for me. Or to confirm the rumours."

The next kiss diverged miles away from sweet as he swept his tongue into her mouth. Nothing had ever felt as exquisite as she accepted him and responded. Her core pulsed as she inhaled the heady scent of his natural scent accented with soap.

He broke off the kiss, but his hands kept rubbing up and down her back. "Will you make love to me?"

She blinked several times as she stared into his eyes. It had been the first time she'd been asked. Things had naturally tended to progress in that direction with other men.

A sense of euphoria filled her at how much he respected her, and she wanted him even more.

She lay a hand against his cheek. "Yes."

Air rushed from Akin's lungs in relief at the single word. Capturing her luscious mouth once again, he took his time savouring her. They had the rest of the night. A tightness clamped his chest. This would the only night they'd have together.

Pushing the melancholy away, he strove to live in the moment. With Comfort. Joining their bodies in a way so that she'd always know how much she'd come to mean to him. What would they become if they had more time?

Releasing her lips, he reached out and unbuttoned the top of her uniform, leaving her with a white T-shirt.

His stomach quivered when she reached under the hem of his shirt and slid her hands up along his ribs.

"Help me take it off," she ordered.

Without hesitation, he snagged it off. She stepped into his space and licked, then nipped his right pec as she skimmed her fingers along his arms.

The heat of her breath fanned along his nipple when she whispered, "Make love to me, Akin."

He stripped them both naked as they kissed and caressed each other with increasing desperation.

With regret, he let her go and lifted his rack. He reached in and scrounged through his roughsack. Finding the box of condoms, he opened it and removed one.

Raising his gaze to Comfort, he froze as the lush beauty of her naked form hit him. How could one woman be so amazing on so many levels?

She came to him and grabbed the condom.

"Need help?" She tore the packet open.

His eyes crossed, and he moaned as she eased the protection onto him.

Once they were settled on the mattress, he closed the curtain around them. The world disappeared. Lying beneath him, she responded with her hips and intoxicating sounds of pleasure as he stroked her slick core.

She held his face still and looked him in the eyes. "Now. I need you now."

With one smooth motion, he eased into her heat. The sense of being home had never been more prominent.

They clung to each other as they set a concordant rhythm. When her inner walls spasmed around him, she dragged him with her into a world of pure ecstasy.

Returning to reality, he kissed her glistening forehead, cheeks, nose, chin, and her soft, sweet lips and pushed away thoughts of how much it would devastate him to lose her.

He slid out of her tight sheath only to have her whimper at the loss of their connection, making him crave to delve back in.

Did she feel it, too? How much they belonged together? What would he give to keep her by his side?

The sea.

CHAPTER TWENTY-THREE

Comfort struggled to breathe with Akin's full weight on her. The second time they'd made love had been even more soul-searing than the first. Their bodies had fit together so perfectly, it had brought tears to her eyes.

After a moment, he pushed up on his arms. She held on tight with her legs and arms, never wanting to let go of the moment. To let go of him.

"I'm crushing you," he said with a huskiness that vibrated in her chest.

"I don't care."

He rolled onto his side with her still clutching him. "There are too many people on this ship who'd make me walk the plank if anything happened to you."

"Do they really do that?"

Having shocked her into relaxing her grip, he pulled out of her. Before knowing him, she'd never felt so empty after being so filled.

He chuckled and rubbed his nose against hers with a quick kiss to her lips. How could such a stern man be this affectionate? She loved how he'd touched her in the gentlest of ways over the past few hours. She couldn't get enough of him. How would she survive leaving him?

She traced the edges of his mouth with her finger before relishing in the soft texture with her lips. If she hadn't fallen already, then she was well on her way. No amount of logical thinking could release her from the truth. It was a miracle how something she hadn't been looking for had found its way so irrevocably into her life.

Yet, with all the loss she'd endured, the lives she'd seen snatched away from this Earth, she had no doubt that what she felt for him was real and true. She didn't know a whole lot about him other than he was honest, intelligent, disciplined, respected, and so tender that it made her heart hurt.

With a peck to her cheek and a smile, he climbed over her and got out of the bed to take care of their protection. She followed him out and picked up his T-shirt. When she put it on, it fell to the middle of her thighs and smelled like him. Reassuring. She tucked herself back into his bunk.

He stepped into a pair of shorts, got into the bed, and covered them with the blanket. Separation wasn't an option.

Curling up against him, she lay her head on his chest. Silent moments of bliss passed before he spoke.

"Why didn't you tell me that Umale had been bothering you?"

She propped herself to a half-seated position. After a sexual experience she was sure had changed her life, that's what he wanted to talk about? "How'd you find out?"

"Dubem told me."

Infuriated with the Executive Officer, she released words she should've kept in. "Did he tell you that his approach was worse, because he tried to make me think I was crazy when he did the same?"

Akin jumped out of bed and reached for his pants. How the hell hadn't he banged his head against the top bunk during the manoeuvre?

"My gut told me he hadn't been joking. I'm going to kill him. And then, I'm going for Umale."

She stood and ran to the door before he could reach it. Not that her physical barrier would do any good if he really wanted to leave.

"That's why I didn't tell you. Creating situations of bloodshed isn't my thing." She placed a hand on his still bare chest as his breaths came in short pants. "Besides, I handled both of them. They haven't even tried to look at me in days."

For the most part.

He seemed to calm as she swept her hands to his shoulders and started massaging. The distraction was having an arousing effect on her body that she hadn't anticipated.

"We have one night together. Do you really want to spend it fighting with them?" She stepped closer so that her hardened nipples pressed into him. She then rose onto her toes and nibbled his earlobe. "Or making love to me?"

He slammed his lips down onto hers as he pulled her hips close.

He'd made the right decision.

Comfort's stomach had complained of hunger as they'd lain in bed entwined in each other. The protein bar he'd given her had been filling, if not tasty. Now cuddled into his side, it was her turn to bring up something that was upsetting her.

"Ishaq told me you enlisted in the navy at the same time. He's looking forward to retiring this year."

Unable to ask if he had the same plans, she let the unspoken words ping around in her mind, hoping he'd developed telepathic powers.

When he didn't speak, she sucked in a breath and released a sigh. She'd have to be direct. "Are you going to retire, too?"

He kissed the top of her head, and she shivered with the deliciousness of the gesture.

"One day."

"Oh."

"I had never really questioned staying in the navy until I absolutely had to retire." He squeezed her tight. "Until I got to know you."

"Oh," she repeated with a more hopeful note as she recalled that he'd never considered leaving the navy for his ex-wife. "But I'm not enough."

Her words hung heavy. She had her answer with his silence.

"What will you do when we get to Lagos?" he finally asked.

Had she thought she could end up with him? They'd known each other for basically no time at all. She'd been irrational to think that maybe, they had a chance. Their lives were too different to comprehend being together. He loved the navy, and she... Not a single idea came to mind when it came to her future. It had been so long since she'd envisioned having one. Running and hiding from herself and her past had been her reason for joining MSF.

Now that she'd faced her demons and was on her way to accepting them, what would she do with her life? Continue to work in war-torn and epidemic-ridden areas helping people? Had the work fulfilled her? Had anything?

Akin had. For the days they'd been together and actually gotten along, she'd been happy and almost sure about her place. And now, she had no idea.

"I'll join up with MSF and see where that takes me."

"Have you ever thought about settling down?"

She snorted. "Isn't that like the pot calling the bottom of the kettle black?"

She grimaced, not having meant to say it in as harsh a tone as it had come out.

Her head shifted at his shrug.

"I want you to be safe."

Didn't she want the same for him? Him fighting pirates, no matter how good they were at it, wouldn't help her to sleep well at night.

"I've survived this long. I'll be okay."

She'd be heartbroken without him, but she'd get over it and survive. At least, her bouts of depression hadn't killed her.

He changed their positions so they lay on their sides on the small mattress, facing each other. "Where will you be staying in Lagos?"

She hadn't thought about it. "A hotel for a few days until I get organized with MSF. I've never been to Nigeria. I'd like to tour the city."

His eyes glittered. "Would you like to stay at my home?"

With her heart beating a little faster, the smile spread across her face before she could stop it.

Just as quickly, the bliss she'd felt seconds before plummeted like a dropped bowling ball. What good would staying with him do? She'd fall completely in love with him, making it even more painful when he left her for the sea or she returned to her work with MSF.

This would truly be their last night together. An anchor sitting on her chest couldn't have made breathing any more difficult.

"It would be better if I didn't."

His Adam's apple bobbed with his swallow as he nodded. Did he understand? Even if he didn't, she'd made the right decision. But they still had these last few hours alone.

Climbing on top of him, she kissed him, hoping he knew how much she cared. How much she'd miss him. Forever.

CHAPTER TWENTY-FOUR

Comfort watched Ancille hang up the wall phone in the sick bay the next morning. He looked at her. "Captain would like to see you."

Her eyes went wide at the summons.

Ishaq grinned. "It's probably to thank you for your service."

"Oh." She headed to the door, only to be followed by Ancille. She pivoted, ready to tell him to stay.

Ishaq's laughter had him clutching his abdomen. "I've noticed you have no sense of direction. I don't want you falling off the ship before we get you safely to shore."

"Smartass."

She'd miss him and the rest of the crew. All except the ones who'd given her a hard time. Pushing it aside, she followed Ancille through the passageways and up the metal ladder she'd learned not to fear tumbling down. She could even descend them while facing forward instead of arse first.

Having reached the captain's office, she knocked on the steel.

"Come in."

The captain looked up from whatever he'd been working on and waved a hand to the chairs in front of the desk. "Have a seat."

"Thank you, sir."

The butterflies had started a violent dance in her belly. Why should she be nervous? He held a different type of power than Akin. One not as overt, yet still present. He wouldn't be someone she'd ever want to cross.

Captain Obot linked his fingers on his desk. "I called you here to thank you for your service."

"It was my pleasure, sir."

He nodded. "No, indeed, the pleasure was ours. Ishaq mentioned that the men trusted you enough to make you a confidant."

"Listening is a big part of being a doctor, sir."

Damn her training. She hadn't been in the military for years, and yet, facing him, she couldn't end a sentence without the word sir. Not even the meaner aspect of Akin had elicited such a response from her.

"What are your plans?"

The same question Akin had asked her last night. Heat flushed her skin at the memory of them merging into one.

"I think I'll go back to the UK for a while to figure out what I want to do with my life."

She'd realized as she lay in Akin's arms, listening to his steady heartbeat, that she was drained. Tired of grieving for her family and lost marriage. Tired of trying to outrun herself. Tired of not living.

"You have my condolences on the loss of your family."

Of course, he'd known. Where was his uncomfortable shifting in the seat? The aversion of looking into her eyes? The pity?

"Thank you."

"Someone mentioned that your parents were from Ghana. What about your extended family? Could you go to them?"

"I was born and raised in the UK. I met my larger family once on a family vacation to Ghana when I was ten."

His gaze probed into her. "I see. What's in the UK for you to return to?"

Was it his intention to make her cry? Yet, the ingrained respect for those older than her from both her parents and those higher in rank from the army reserves prevented her from telling him it was none of his business.

His eyes softened. "I'm not trying to pry. I'd like to help if I can."

"I need to sort out my life. To find out where I'm supposed to be. I think the UK might be the best place to do it."

"What about Solarin?"

She couldn't help the gasp the sharp intake of air produced. What did the man know about her and his Commander of Warfare?

"What about him, sir?"

Captain Obot chuckled.

"It's not a secret. I've seen you two together. I've known him for the better part of his career, and I've never seen him as besotted with someone, even his ex-wife, as he is with you." He narrowed his eyes as if attempting to see through her. "Correct me if I'm wrong, but you seem happier now—at least you did yesterday—than when you initially stepped onto my ship."

She'd admit to no such thing. Even if it were the truth. If she weren't leaving Akin, she'd probably be floating after the blissful night they'd spent together.

He was everything she'd ever wanted in a man. The kind who'd stick with her through thick and thin. If he were hers, she wouldn't be able to drive him away even if she wanted to. To those he was dedicated to, he'd stand by. Unfortunately, the navy alone held his heart and devotion.

Captain Obot breathed out a sigh through his nose. "As you well know, this is my ship. As captain, for the safety of my crew, I make it my business to know everything that goes on."

Sure that her face was flaming red, she attempted to maintain a neutral expression. He couldn't know about how she'd had to bite Akin's shoulder to stave off a scream as she'd climaxed last night and this morning. How she'd started mourning the loss of him in her life when she'd had to release him from the hug they'd shared before leaving the cabin to go to work.

"Well, most of the things. I hope you'll listen to some advice from an old man."

She clasped her hands together, sure that nothing other than the ship being attacked would stop him from speaking his mind.

"I've seen and experienced a lot in my lifetime. Both horrific and beautiful. You being a doctor and a survivor, I don't need to tell you how short life is. My advice is that you live it."

She waited for him to say more. To tell her to claim Akin as hers no matter how little they knew about each other. To settle for a life where he'd spend more time on his precious ocean than he would with her. To give whatever swirled between them a chance. To let her heart rule her life because it would never steer her wrong.

He said none of those. Standing, he saluted her.

Honoured and humbled, she stood and returned it.

"Once again, thank you for your service. You will do well in life, Dr. Comfort Djan. Take care of yourself. If our paths cross again, it will be a positive thing."

She blinked back the burn in her eyes. No need to embarrass herself. "Thank you for trusting that I would serve you and your men well, sir."

She turned and headed for the door.

"One last thing."

She pivoted. "Yes, sir."

He held out an envelope, which she went back to take.

"You are always welcome aboard this ship."

"Thank you, sir."

She rushed out before he could witness the tears. Not even in the UK had she ever felt so accepted at work. The crew had made her feel part of the tight-knit family they'd created.

Akin. She cared about him. Deeply. How did he feel about her? Would he ever be willing to give them a chance, or had he given up on ever falling in love with anything but his career? The questions crowded her mind.

If they knew each other better, she'd take the risk and ask, but she didn't. Her heart was still too fragile, and rejection would most likely destroy her.

Akin knew how to speak his mind. If he wanted her, he'd let her know. Yes, he'd invited her to stay at his home, but it wasn't enough. As ridiculous as it sounded, even in her head, nothing but his declaration of love, or at least him claiming to care for her, would be.

Seeing how unlikely that was, she'd leave. She'd find her way, and as the captain had advised her to do, she'd live. Broken-hearted, but she'd live.

CHAPTER TWENTY-FIVE

By the time she'd extracted herself from her meandering thoughts, Comfort had found that she'd walked a couple of minutes down a passageway devoid of any of the men who'd guarded her while she'd been on board. Ancille must have thought she'd be meeting with the captain longer than she had and returned to sick bay to finish taking stock and locking up the supplies with Ishaq. They'd almost been done by the time she'd been called.

Had she turned a corner or two? She couldn't remember.

She could either return to sick bay, or she could go to her room and pack since they'd be pulling into port in less than thirty minutes. For someone who moved a lot, she absolutely hated packing, so the dilemma was real. She'd been avoiding it all day and now had to get it done.

She headed in the direction of her room, occasionally distracted by the waves to the men, already dressed in their navy whites and caps and ready to disembark. She envied the ones who had people waiting for their return.

Her muscles stiffened as the hairs at the back of her neck rose and her ears perked up at the cackle of laughter. Not a pleasant sound. She looked behind her, to find the space empty. After taking the stairs down and rounding a couple of corners, she should've been at her room.

The numbers and letters on the sign whose mission was to announce her location didn't look familiar. As she contemplated which way would lead her to her room, or even the sick bay, she recognized some of the sailors who'd frowned at her when she'd initially boarded the ship and on the first day she'd eaten at the Mess. Her instincts went on high alert as her heart started to race. She'd broken the single promise she'd made to Akin. Now, she was alone with men who hadn't wanted her on their vessel in the first place.

She made a right turn and hoped she'd meet up with someone who actually liked her. Or was at least neutral to her presence. The metal door in front of her screamed dead end.

"Doc," one of the men said as their footsteps got closer.

She turned and stood in a stance that would allow her to fight if it came down to it. She could take them on. Or at least bring a couple down with her.

"What are you doing down in the laundry room area?" one of the men asked. "Didn't they return your things to you? Do you need to get inside? We were coming to make sure the place was locked up. If you need to get something, we could let you in."

He sounded friendly. Even helpful, but she didn't relax.

Before she could answer, the shortest of the three asked, "Where's Commander Solarin?"

She looked into each of their faces, searching for ill intent. She found none. "Waiting for me. I may have gotten a little turned around."

"You mean lost."

The group laughed at her expense, and she joined them.

The men turned and left the short hallway and then waited for her to follow.

"Where are you going? We'll escort you. It's the least we can do for coming on board the ship when we needed you."

"And for saving Doc's life like you did. He's the closest some of us have ever had to a father. Always willing to listen when we need him."

One of the guys elbowed another. "And give us antibiotics for those times when we're in a pinch."

The group laughed again.

Had she been mistaken when she'd taken their grimaces as animosity towards her that first day when it could've been concern for their comrade instead?

"I'd like to go back to my room."

They told her what they'd be doing during their two-week leave as they walked in the opposite direction she'd come.

"Thanks for escorting me back."

"Anytime," the one she'd consider the leader said.

As if choreographed, they saluted her before going.

She let herself into the room, getting mentally prepared to pack when she all she wanted to crawl into Akin's bed and wait for him.

By the time the two men lunged towards her, it was too late.

Reckoning had been docked at the Lagos Port for about fifteen minutes by the time Akin had ensured that the men had completed their assigned duties. The tasks had taken longer than usual due to the extensive inventory they'd had to do. They'd whooped and clapped when he'd dismissed them to go for their leave.

He stopped by the sick bay to find it locked. Ishaq must have sent Comfort back to the room after they'd finished their work. His heart raced at the anticipation of seeing her again.

He hadn't seen her since they'd left the room later than usual that morning. Making love to her that last time had filled him with a completion so great that he didn't know how he'd ever be able to say goodbye. When they'd come down from their orgasmic high, reality and responsibilities had intruded. They'd showered and had gotten dressed without saying much.

They'd shared a bittersweet embrace. He'd never wanted to let her go, but he knew he couldn't keep her. Not without losing a vital part of himself.

He entered their room expecting to smell her enticing floral scent and look into her brilliant eyes. The space was empty. Her bed had been stripped. The sheets, blanket, and pillow case sat folded at the bottom of the bunk.

Not accepting what his senses told him, he lifted the bunk. The clothes had been removed.

The suitcase she'd placed in the corner of the room was also missing.

His mind raced. Maybe she'd gone to the Mess. Logic told him she wouldn't be there because they had closed down after lunch. Why hadn't he joined her for the meal instead of sending a message to Ishaq to take her?

When he opened the door to the Mess, it was as he'd suspected. Empty except for the familiar benches and tables. He jiggled the door to the kitchen. Locked. Taking the chance, he knocked anyway. No answer.

She could be hanging out with Ishaq, helping him prepare to leave and saying her goodbyes. Akin headed to his friend's room. Instead of knocking, he opened the metal. Ishaq alone sat at his desk, writing in a notebook.

Unless she was behind the door. She wasn't there.

"Where's Comfort?"

"Isn't she in the cabin?" Ishaq asked. "She'd complained about having to pack."

Rubbing the back of his neck, Akin paced the room. "No. Not in the Mess, either, and as you know, the sick bay is locked."

Ishaq's brows furrowed. "That was the last time place I saw her. She'd been called to Captain's office. Ancille had escorted her there."

Akin rotated on his heel. "Didn't he return with her?"

"He came back alone. I thought the captain had dismissed him and would call someone else to walk her back."

He poked a finger hard into his chest. "That's my job. Captain wouldn't think of it."

As he was pulling the door open, his friend's question stopped him from storming out.

"Where are you going?"

"To the captain's office."

"What if she disembarked?"

That was harder to answer. His voice came out gruff.

"She wouldn't leave without saying goodbye."

He spoke the truth as he knew it. After losing her family unexpectedly, she'd never leave him without obtaining closure, no matter what had happened between them.

Walking the passageways at a fast clip, he came inches from barrelling someone over. Umale. What was he still doing on board? Logistics had been the first of the crew to disembark. If he wasn't worried about Comfort's whereabouts, he'd find a way to have him punished. It didn't matter for what. The fact that he'd been a bother to Comfort was enough for him. The smirk the boy added to his salute didn't sit well as Akin rushed off. Disrespectful bastard.

He knocked on the captain's door. No answer. He repeated the action with the same response. Maybe the man had taken Comfort to the bridge.

Taking the stairs two at a time, he saw the captain and a few crew members completing their work. Comfort wasn't among them.

He saluted the captain. "I was looking for Dr. Djan, sir."

"I spoke to her in my office about forty-five minutes ago. She's a special woman, Akin."

He'd just been told something he'd already realized and had been fool enough to almost let go. He'd rectify the situation as soon as he yelled at her for scaring the hell out of him by going AWOL. "She is, sir."

"I'm glad you recognise it. Have a good break."

Dismissed, he left the bridge. His mind worked overtime wondering where she could be. Maybe she'd taken one last tour of the ship before returning. He refused to believe that she'd left. She wouldn't.

He returned to the cabin and assessed the room. Opening his curtain, he found the bunk in the same neat state he'd left it. He raised it. Everything was in order. He did the same for the other three racks. Empty.

Hands on hips, he examined the deck. Something white caught his eye, peeping out from under his bunk. He bent and pulled it out. An unopened envelope. He turned it over to find it addressed to Comfort in the captain's angular script. She would never have left this behind.

What if it had slipped off her bed? He refused to believe the thought.

The woman travelled the world with a suitcase of memorabilia. She would have taken great care with the letter.

Her suitcase. It was still in storage where he'd signed it in. It had to be. No one was allowed to take anything out on another's behalf.

Rather than follow the rules and walk, he jogged to the storage area which would be the last department on the ship to close.

"The suitcase. Is it here?"

The sailor who'd been present when he'd dropped it off blinked up at him. "Yes, sir. You haven't signed it out."

He bit his cheek at the jolt of foreboding which ripped through him. Unable to celebrate the fact that she hadn't left him, his mind raced to figure out her location.

"Give it to me."

He signed the paper, and the attendant scurried to retrieve the luggage.

Where the hell was she?

CHAPTER TWENTY-SIX

Comfort struggled to untie the rope binding her wrists to the chair. An impossibility considering that a sailor had tied them. The screams she attempted came out as muffles through the gag.

If the bastards hadn't jumped her using a stun gun, things would've turned out much differently. Her arm and leg muscles flexed at the memory of having electricity shot into her. She'd never experienced anything more physically debilitating as she'd lost control of her muscles. The inch her head had been spared from the edge of the bunk had been pure luck. She'd landed on her shoulder, buffering the impact of her head hitting the deck.

She'd willed herself to fight as her captors had bound and gagged her before shoving her into a sack. Her muscles had been too weak from their sudden forced exertion. Slung over a shoulder, she'd been carried until they'd reached the room she was currently being held in. Not once had her captors spoken.

The only light in the room seeped in from under the door. The only time she'd been able to see had been when her abductor had opened the door to leave, locking her in. Shelves filled with cleaning supplies lined one set of walls. A mass of toiletry products took up its own space, while articles she hadn't been able to identify filled the rest of the shelves.

Anger roiled through her as she worked at untying the ropes. It was the only emotion she'd allow. Fear wasn't an option, nor was it necessary. Akin would find her. It may be after she'd ripped out the bastards' throats, but he'd find her.

The suitcase she'd glimpsed sitting to the right of her gave her pause. If Akin thought she'd left the ship, would he search for her? Their talk hadn't ended well last night.

They'd both known they had no future together, so they'd appreciated the sensual moments they'd had remaining.

She shook off the doubt attempting to creep in and freak her out. Akin would know that she'd never leave him without saying goodbye. Not after the way her family had been stolen from her. She held out hope that he'd find her sooner rather than later.

If only she could see better, she'd hunt for something which could be used to get her out of the ropes. Anything with a serrated edge would do. A knife would be best, but she might be pushing things considering she was bound.

She forced the legs they'd tied together to lift the chair. Failure. Inching it towards the door had yielded no results. It was too heavy.

The sound of an announcement stilled her efforts to attack the ropes agitating her wrists.

"Dr. Comfort Djan, report to the captain's office."

The captain repeated the sentence twice more. Her chest sank at her relieved exhale. She held back a sob. Akin knew she was missing, and he'd find her.

Once he discovered the identities of her captors...she wouldn't even think of the carnage he'd wreak. She grunted as she imagined how she'd help him.

Akin paced the tiny space of the captain's office with the other commanders as they waited for Comfort to show up. After sprinting to the gangway and discovering from the ensign that she hadn't left the ship, he'd asked if any of the men had carried out an abnormally large bag or if a crate had gone out. The man couldn't recall any, but he wasn't a hundred percent sure.

When he'd requested for the CCTV footage, he'd been told that they'd been ordered by Commander Lewis to do checks on the system because of a glitch they'd experienced earlier in the day. It had been offline for the past three hours.

His stomach had sunk. The recordings would've told him everything. If she'd been abducted from the ship to Lagos, he had no idea how he'd find her. With cell phones now working, he had called the captain to pipe for Comfort to get to his office. He'd ordered the ensign to close the gate to the gangplank and not let anyone else off or onto the ship until instructed to do so by either him or the captain.

His first inclination was to tear through the ship himself looking for her. It would be an extensive venture. He'd need help; yet, who could he trust other than Ishaq? With the way Dubem had lusted after her, he'd been crossed off the list as trustworthy. Any of the men could've taken her and stowed her somewhere. *Reckoning* held more crevices than a human brain. She could be anywhere.

Akin watched as the fifty-plus men present divided themselves into search teams of two. Although Ishaq had been raring to join the search, Akin had insisted he sit it out. He assigned each group to search an area they were familiar with.

"Be thorough." He added bass to his voice to relay the importance of the mission. "Dr. Djan is on this ship and will be found."

The men scuttled off.

Lewis sidled up to him. "Don't worry, Solarin. If the lady is on the ship, she'll come up. Why do you think she hasn't gone ashore with another sailor?"

He clenched his jaw. The same instinct which told him that Comfort wouldn't leave told him not to inform Lewis about the suitcase he'd kept in storage. "It's not like her to take off."

"But you've known her for less than a week. How do you know what she'd do? She was sniffling and wiping her eyes from what looked like tears when I saw her leaving the captain's office before docking." He set his lips into a frown. "She's a good woman. Proud, too. Maybe she took off to manage her emotions. Think about that."

Umale left with Lewis. Akin balled his fists when the boy's smirk resembled the one he'd given him earlier.

That was odd. Why would Lewis and Umale team up? They weren't friends or in the same clique, although Umale was under Lewis in Logistics.

As if on auto-pilot, Akin walked in the direction the two had taken.

What was Umale still doing on the ship? He often helped open the gate so that he could be one of the first out. For him to have hovered so long made no sense.

Akin kept himself hidden from the two as he tailed them. Lewis calling Comfort a lady had set off a warning bell. He'd never heard him use that word. Bitches, sluts, hoes, whores, any negative derivative a person could think of—Lewis had used it. Never lady.

The duo turned in the direction towards where they'd been assigned. They hadn't opened a single door they'd passed as they reached the end of the passageway and spoke with their heads together.

Akin barely held himself in place as he stood in a space where he could watch them through the mirror without them seeing him until they were closer. Ten minutes passed, and he wanted to knock their skulls together for wasting so much time.

Umale's laziness knew no bounds, but he wouldn't have guessed it of Lewis. The two were up to something. If it had anything to do with Comfort's disappearance, they might not live to regret it.

When they started back towards his direction, he slipped into a berthing until he heard them pass. He took another passageway and met them at the captain's office giving their report like the others.

"We checked everywhere." Lewis waved a hand to indicate the room. "Looks like nobody found her. With all due respect, sir, I believe she left the ship. Can I suggest that you let the rest of us follow suit so that we can enjoy our short break? It's been a stressful tour with Ishaq almost dying and the two pirate apprehensions. I'm sure the men are ready for their R and R."

Rest and relaxation, his arse.

"I think you're right, Lewis. Dr. Djan and I had an argument this morning, so maybe she just wanted to escape." He turned to the captain. "We have her contact information through MSF. We can reach her by phone."

"Are you sure, Akin?" Dubem asked. "We can do another run-through of different sections just in case anyone missed anything."

Dubem was the last person he would've expected to make the offer. Perhaps he was covering his own involvement. Or maybe he had nothing to do with her disappearance and wanted to find her.

Never one to hesitate when making a decision, the captain agreed with a curt nod. "Thank you all for your help. You are dismissed."

Lewis' grin set off a tick in Akin's cheek. "Thank you, Captain."

He left the area, and once again, Umale followed.

Akin asked Ishaq to get Comfort's information from the captain, then he trailed after Lewis and Umale. If either of them knew of Comfort's whereabouts, they'd lead him right to her.

He wouldn't worry yet about if they didn't.

CHAPTER TWENTY-SEVEN

Comfort hunched in the chair, exhausted as blood dripped over her fingers. When she'd heard men talking in the hallway, she'd tried her best to lift the chair so that she could make enough noise to be heard. No luck. By the time she'd gotten the chair to make a tiny squeak, the voices had gone.

She refused to panic. If Akin couldn't get her out of the situation, then she would. Living life to the fullest was now high on her priorities' roster, and she wouldn't let anyone interfere.

After what felt like hours, the door opened, and Umale strode in, locking the door behind him. Despite the pain of broken skin, she attempted to work on the ropes again.

"Not so in control, are you, bitch."

The breaths she took through her nose came so rapidly that she became dizzy. She made an attempt to tamper down her dread by strategizing ways of taking him out. Her breathing slowed.

"I've been given permission to use you for a few hours." He snorted. "As if I wouldn't, anyway."

Her eyes widened at his maniacal laugh. The same she'd heard when she'd walked in the passageway earlier.

"Not only do I get to take what you wouldn't give, but I'm making money off it, too." He put his face in hers before moving to her ear and biting it until it hurt. "I won't make it good for you like I promised before. It will hurt, and you will scream, or try to, anyway. No one will hear you, but I'll know."

He held her head still as he placed his mouth over the gag and blew so hard that air rushed into her mouth.

Her heart couldn't be calmed as easily as her breath while she turned her head from his.

He grabbed her breasts and twisted. She refused to release the whimper of pain he'd caused.

She wouldn't give him the satisfaction of getting off on it.

"Tough, aren't you. Even if I can't break you, which I'm going to have good time doing, the pirates we're selling you to sure will. You won't have the chance to say no as they plow you all day every day."

Tears rolled down her cheek thinking about the torture she'd meet if she didn't get herself away from this insane man. He swiped them away and licked his finger.

"They're paying extra for your medical skills. I didn't see how they'd make you treat them, but Commander explained it in graphic detail. You'll do as they say." He reached down, cupped between her legs, and squeezed. "It's a win-win. At least for me. You'll live and die a life of Hell. Pirates are not known for their kindness. And neither am I. It serves Solarin right. Bastard ruined my progress, so I'm going to destroy his girl."

The cackle returned, clawing against her ear drums.

"Too bad he'll never learn what happened to you. Poor little orphaned girl. There's nobody to miss you. Nobody to look for you. Solarin won't even think about you once he gets off this ship. He gave up the search easily, too. The fact that I'll know where you are and that you're getting what your snooty arse deserves will be enough."

He leaned over her and bit the side of her neck so hard that she couldn't hold back a whine.

"You're a perfect cash cow. Commander is right—women are useless whores who deserve nothing more than to be used, tossed aside, and used another day."

He unbuckled his belt and undid the button of his trousers. "I'm going to make this really special. For me."

Lewis had gone towards his office while Umale had walked alone down a passageway. Since it was unlikely that they'd hold Comfort in an office, he followed Umale.

The boy opened the door to the supply room on the first level. Before Akin could rush the door, Umale had closed and locked it. He stood for a moment listening. The bastard started speaking.

Comfort.

Akin was strong, but the metal was built to sustain a force much greater than he could apply. Two other people had a key to the closet. He'd be damned if he'd go to Lewis.

Sprinting to the captain's office, he broke protocol by ignoring the man and searching the cabinet for the supply room key. They were easy to find in their alphabetical order.

Stripping off his uniform, he wrapped his elbow with it. He broke the glass with a single strike before pulling out the key.

"Send men to the first floor supply room. Now," he ordered the captain before sprinting out.

In record time, he reached the supply room, stuck the key in, and burst through the door. It took a moment for his eyes to adjust to the dimness.

When he did, the scene resembled a slow-motion movie.

"You bitch."

Umale charged towards Comfort. She bent her legs towards her chest, and at the perfect moment, propelled them out. Her power sent Umale flying into the metal brackets holding the shelves. He hit his head and crumbled to the ground.

Over his shock, Akin rushed in and grabbed Umale and flipped him onto his back. Straddling the still-conscious young man, he wrapped his hands around the skinny throat and squeezed. He found a great satisfaction in the boy's eyes bugging out as he clawed at his forearms.

Stomping broke through his rage, and he looked up to see Comfort with tears streaming down her cheeks, shaking her head to give her abductor mercy.

If he killed Umale, the bastard could never bother her again. The thought had him squeezing harder until her frantic mumble through the gag reached into him.

Hadn't she been through enough?

Akin released his quarry just as two sailors ran into the room.

"Sir," one of them breathed.

He released his grip.

Umale shrieked in a breath and began to cough.

Akin stood. Accidentally kicking Umale in the ribs with his steel-toed boots, he stalked towards Comfort.

He untied her legs and threw the rope at the sailors. "Tie him up and watch him."

As he removed the gag from Comfort's mouth, Dubem ran in.

He took in the scene. Eyes rounded and mouth open, he stumbled back as his gaze landed on Umale lying on the floor between the men. Either he was an Oscar-worthy actor, or he'd had absolutely no idea about the abduction.

"What's going on?"

Comfort ignored him as she panted. "Lewis. Arrest him. He's working with Umale."

Akin had a decision to make. Stay by her side and assign the task to Dubem, or go after Lewis.

"Dubem," he ordered with a flick of his head towards the door.

The man nodded and took off with two of the sailors who had crowded in with him.

He moved behind Comfort, and rage flared at her bleeding wrists. He made short work of undoing the knots and removing the rope. When she stood and reached for him, he pulled her into his arms and held tight.

"It's about damn time," she whispered with a sob.

His knees weakened with relief as he held her. "Tell Ishaq to meet us at sick bay. He should call an ambulance."

"Ignore the part about the ambulance," she ordered. "I don't need one. These are abrasions. I can treat them myself."

He released her and held onto her shoulders as he looked into her eyes. "Did he hurt you?"

"No," she said in a strong voice.

Her vengeance was a work of art as she swerved around him and ran towards where Umale had been brought to stand with his hands tied behind his back. Her flying side kick landed straight in Umale's groin, driving him onto his arse.

She landed hard on her feet. "I hope that was special enough for you, mother fu—"

Umale's delayed scream of pain blocked out her words as she cussed him out. Akin grabbed her from behind and lifted her as she charged towards Umale with her hands at his throat level.

Akin didn't bother to hold back his smile. He'd never have to worry about his woman's safety. Ever.

CHAPTER TWENTY-EIGHT

Hours after they'd found her, Comfort could barely keep her eyes open. The debriefing with the captain had taken forever. She'd explained what had happened. And then, he'd proceeded to ask her the same questions in different ways in order to ascertain the truth of her report. If she'd been lying, she had no doubt she'd have been caught.

They'd had a naval IT specialist come on board and had thus gained access to Lewis' computer when he'd refused to provide the password. The spreadsheet they'd found of payments made to him by various groups considered to be outlaws helped corroborate Comfort's story of his involvement. If she ever saw the man again and had a stun gun on hand, she wouldn't hesitate to use it.

Where Umale's motive of money, power, and revenge was clear, Lewis' wasn't.

"It has to be money," Akin said. "With you being a woman, he had an added motivation to appease his misogynistic personality." He shook his head. "What I can't figure out is why none of us caught it."

She raised a hand to cover her yawn and ignored the bandages that Ishaq had wrapped around her wrists. She'd be changing them for weeks to come.

"How could you have known? He hid his nefarious activities well."

She'd sensed the coldness in him the first day they'd met, but she'd never have guessed he would've taken things as far as he had.

Akin had asked her to stay with him at his home just outside of Lagos. Not wanting to be without him, she'd agreed. From the moment they'd sat in his Jeep, she'd fallen asleep.

"Comfort, wake up. We've arrived."

Her eyes shot open as fear clenched her heart at the unfamiliarity of her environment.

"It's okay. You're safe." Akin's voice was as soothing as a soft caress.

She leaned her head against the back of her seat with relief. When she was ready to leave the sanctuary of the vehicle, she pulled the latch and opened the door.

By the time she'd closed it, Akin hovered near. Her body couldn't resist leaning against him as they walked to the house.

They stepped into his home when the door was opened for them by a boy the age of sixteen or so. She greeted him with a weak smile.

"You took a shower on the ship, but would you like to soak in a bath here?"

Touched by his consideration, she placed a hand on his stubbled cheek. "Sleep, please. Tomorrow, bath."

If she ever woke up. She'd never suffered such a state of fatigue. Then again, she'd never been electrocuted, kidnapped, mentally tortured, nearly raped and sold to pirates to be a sex slave, either. It had been an unimaginable day.

"Are you hungry?"

"No."

Step by step, she followed him as they ascended. He opened the first door at the right of the staircase. The room was done in various states of beige and devoid of any personal items. It wasn't his room.

She shook her head and backed out. "Is your room so messy that I can't sleep in it?"

He laughed and led her down the hallway. It was odd not to have the floor sway beneath her. Something she hadn't noticed while on the ship. They entered a room that screamed masculine with its navy blue bedspread and hardwood floors. His things were organized in straight lines on the dresser, and the place was spotless.

The boy she'd met downstairs knocked on the open door. Akin grabbed the suitcases from him and brought them into the room.

"Do you want me to get your pyjamas for you?" he asked.

"I want your T-shirt."

He hesitated a moment before going to his dresser and pulling out a white shirt. He handed it to her and then stepped out of the room. She unbuttoned and tugged off her blouse and bra before slipping on the soft cotton. Her trousers were next. After picking up and folding the clothes, she placed them on her suitcase.

Crawling into bed, she hissed when her wrists bent. Snuggling under the sheet, she touched the hurt area. If the abrasions were the worst she'd experienced tonight, then she had angels fighting each other to watch over her and keep her safe. The image made her smile.

Akin had showed up to save her. It was the last thought that drifted through her mind before sinking into a deep sleep.

CHAPTER TWENTY-NINE

Comfort yawned and stretched to her full length. She curled into herself and attempted to get back to the dream the sensation of a full bladder had kicked her out of. Her family had surrounded her, and they'd talked and laughed just like the last day they'd spent together. Before disappearing, they'd reminded her that they'd always be watching over her. A peace had settled into her heart before she'd awoken.

Eyes glued shut, she took her time swinging her feet to the floor and raising her head so she didn't hit it against the top bunk.

Her lids sprang open as the memories of yesterday bombarded her. Heart racing, she jumped out of bed ready to fight as she took in the room.

Akin lay on his side with his head propped on his elbow, as if he'd been watching her.

She let her hands relax at her sides while her pulse settled into a more normal rhythm. "Good morning."

Flutters went off in her stomach at his smile.

"Good morning, Princess."

Suddenly feeling shy, she looked at the floor.

"Where's the head?" She glanced up and giggled. "I meant bathroom."

"Through there."

He pointed to a door she hadn't noticed last night. Stumbling across the room, she entered a bathroom twice the size of the one she'd had in the UK. The patterned tiles sparkled as they met the Jacuzzi, shower, double sink, and toilet. She went to the last and took care of business.

Washing her hands, she noticed her toiletries on the counter. Melting at his thoughtfulness, she brushed her teeth before wrapping her bandaged wrists with the plastic he'd thought to provide. The warm water soothed her when she stepped into the shower. She then grabbed her towel from the rack and dried her body before engulfing herself in the robe hanging against the door.

Refreshed yet still disbelieving about what had happened yesterday, she stared at her reflection. She'd have to face the day and Akin at some point.

She walked into the room to find tantalizing cling-wrapped platters of jollof rice, chicken, fried plantain, and green salad set on the table in the corner. Her stomach grumbled. "For breakfast?"

"It's two in the afternoon. Lunch."

Her eyes bugged. She couldn't remember the last time she'd slept for so long. "I hope you're feeding me Ghanaian jollof. The Nigerian version isn't as good."

Akin's head arched back with his laughter. "I beg to differ. I think you have it the wrong way around."

She shrugged as she sat in front of the food. She had no preference on the country's style of cooking the tomato-stew-infused rice as long as it tasted delicious.

He removed the plastic coverings. After picking up a serving spoon and a plate, he loaded it with jollof. "Tell me when it's enough."

She held out both of her hands. "That's way too much, put some back. Better yet, let me dish it up."

He shifted out of her reach. "Tell me how much you want."

How could she argue with a man wanting to serve her? She instructed him on the quantities and waited for him to serve himself once he'd settled the food in front of her. He sat before she allowed herself to tuck into the food as if she hadn't eaten in days.

The sound of cutlery scraping against teeth and plates were the only sounds in the room until she was content.

"How long has Commander Lewis been insane?"

He considered while chewing.

"He's always been a bit misogynistic, but as sane as the rest of us." He shook his head. "As we discussed last night, I believe greed drove him to get into bed with the pirates. According to that spreadsheet, he'd been embroiled with them for years."

Her stomach churned, threatening to bring up the food she'd just taken in. She pushed her plate away.

"I spoke to Captain this morning." The snap of the chicken bone startled her. "That useless arse Umale confessed to how Lewis had roped him into the venture when he'd heard the rumour of you turning him down. His sadistic ego had been bruised, and he'd wanted vengeance." Akin shook his head. "Not just on you, but me, too. Years ago, I gave him an honest evaluation which prevented him from being promoted in rank."

The muscles in his jaw jumped. "He didn't belong on our ship, but his uncle pulled some strings to get him on."

Her hand flew to her chest. "Lewis is his uncle?"

"Dubem."

Opening her mouth, she could only squeak.

Akin ate a strip of plantain. "By the way, he called, wanting to speak to you. He apologized for his nephew's behaviour and ensured that he would be severely punished by a court of law. He also said that he regretted the way he'd treated you and would stop by to beg your forgiveness in person."

"So he wasn't involved?"

"Not according to the captain. Dubem has a reputation with the ladies. When you paid him no mind, he didn't take it well."

"Too damn bad."

Appetite returning, she ate a forkful of salad.

"What made you search for me?"

"No matter how disappointed you were in me, I knew you wouldn't leave without saying goodbye. I had never signed out the suitcase containing your memorabilia. And…" He got up and went to the bedside table. "I found this in our cabin."

She took it from him. "The envelope that the captain gave me."

"You hadn't opened it. Someone who lugged her past with her all over the world would have taken better care of it."

If she could've, she would've scrambled over the table. Instead, she forced herself to take her time rounding the furniture before throwing herself onto his lap. Despite the short time they'd been acquainted, he knew her.

She grasped the sides of his face and pressed her lips to his. Then, she peppered kisses all over his face, returning to his mouth to show him just how much she cared. When he reached for her breast, pinpricks of fear attacked her skin, and she leapt to her feet.

Umale's hateful words and punishing touch had affected her more than she'd realized. "I need time."

Standing, he offered her his hand. "I understand. Do you want to talk about it?"

She placed her fingers in his offering. He'd become the opposite of the man she'd met. Or maybe, this sweet man had been around the whole time.

"Not right now, but I'll let you know when I'm ready."

Seemingly satisfied with her answer, he squeezed her fingers before letting go and returning to his food. When she sat, he cut a piece of chicken and held it out to her.

"You haven't eaten enough."

"I'm a vegetarian."

His eyes sparkled. "I see. So that side of beef you ate the first meal you had on the ship was, what? An anomaly?"

She chuckled before she opened her mouth to receive the food. She wouldn't have any trouble getting used to being taken care of.

Akin's heart constricted as he watched Comfort finish her salad. For the second time since meeting her, he wished he could undo her past. But then again, wasn't it the previous experiences that made everyone who they are?

If he hadn't met her, his life wouldn't have been irrevocably changed. Which had only occurred because she'd been roaming the globe looking for a peace that he'd been able to help provide her.

Comfort's gentle smile as she read the captain's note lightened his mood. Over time, she'd get over what had happened. He'd make sure to be there for her.

"You realize that you'll have to testify at the trial, right?" he asked once she'd tucked the letter in the envelope.

"I figured."

"The court system here is as slow as coal tar. It might take a few months."

She cocked her head. "You're kidding me!"

"Not at all." He took a sip of his drink in an attempt to settle the nerves firing in his stomach. "I was thinking it would be a good idea for you to stay here with me rather than going off somewhere with MSF where you could miss the court date."

Her eyes sparkled. "Is that so? What would I do in this huge house all alone while you're out to sea?"

He rubbed a finger under his chin. "I haven't taken leave in donkey years. I'm sure I could get a few months off."

"It would be convenient for me to stay here. It's not as if the house is run-down and horrible to look at. I can't imagine being bored around you, either. But what about after the court date and your leave ends?"

"I have my retirement coming up, and I was thinking that it might be time to accept it and stay in one place."

The tears that sprang to her eyes had him clearing his throat.

"You'd give up your career—" She crossed her hands over her chest. "— for me?"

He shrugged. Losing her again wasn't an option he'd entertain.

"That's if we don't end up annoying each other too much in the next few months. Sure, why not."

His attempt to downplay such an important decision wasn't lost on her as she leapt to her feet and once again rounded the table to land herself on his lap.

He accepted her with open arms and held her close as he savoured the delicious texture of her lips. His body stirred, but he kept his hands on neutral areas of her body. She had a lot to deal with, and he'd be patient.

The smile on her face told him he'd made the best decision of his life.

She stretched over the table and picked up the envelope. "The captain offered me a job as the ship's doctor. Of course, I'd have to undertake an intensive specialized navy training."

After what had happened to her, he wanted to add the captain to the list of people he wanted to strangle. He held back his refusal of the job on her behalf.

"After seeing you guys in action, I know that there's no way in hell that a pirate ship could ever get close enough to attack us, so pirates snatching me away isn't an issue."

He remained tense beneath her.

"You've weeded out two of the greedy, mentally unstable people who were on the ship. I can't figure that there'd be many more, especial now that everyone is on high alert."

Her logic made sense even if he still didn't like the idea.

"I could be attacked anywhere. What's the murder rate in Nigeria?"

She had him there, and the kiss she placed on his cheek softened him a bit more.

Comfort looked him in the eyes. "We've been given an opportunity any other sailor would dive for before it slipped away. If we're able to spend the next couple of months without one of us throwing the other out the window, then we won't have to be apart for long stretches of time. As gruff as you can be, I'm pretty sure my stress levels would skyrocket every time you went out to sea."

Her gaze roamed his face and settled on his eyes. "I can't let you give up the career you've worked so hard for and love more than anything else."

Her reasoning had landed on a false point, but he wasn't ready to share it with her yet. Soon, but not yet.

"So what do you say about me taking the job?" she asked, eyes wide and expectant.

"I'll think about it, but for now..." He finished the sentence with a lingering kiss which had her pressing her body closer and his heart soaring.

No matter what decision they made about their careers, they'd be together. Sprinting towards their shared future.

EPILOGUE

Comfort stepped out of the ship's hangar onto the sunlight-drenched deck clinging to Ishaq's solid arm. She smiled even as tears brimmed in her eyes when she saw Akin in his uniform dress whites.

It had taken them nine months to get to this point. Akin's proposal had been the least romantic in history. They'd partnered up and sparred at one of the early morning crew workouts two months ago. He'd taken her down and pinned her until she'd tapped out before hopping onto his feet. He'd reached down to help her up. Pissed that she hadn't been able to deflect the move which had defeated her, she'd slapped his hand away.

When she'd stood glaring at him, he'd thrown his head back and guffawed. Everyone had stopped mid-move and stared. She'd have thought they'd be accustomed to his laughter by then. He did it more often than he had when she'd first met him.

"You're such a sore loser," he'd said. "At least, I know you'll always keep me on my toes. A good quality to have in a wife. Will you marry me?"

She hadn't been the only one to get sea air trapped in their throat. And then, she'd noticed the simple gold banded ring with inlaid diamonds and understood the seriousness of the question.

Jumping up, she'd tackled him to the mats, or at least tried to. He'd caught and held onto her.

"Yes."

When his smile had brightened to the point of nearly blinding her, she'd kissed him.

The men's cheers had been deafening.

As a second and final marriage for both of them, neither had any need for an extravagant ceremony. Just each other, good friends, Akin's family, the sea, and a ship.

In moments, she'd be married to the man she'd fallen irrevocably in love with. Although he didn't say it as often as she liked to hear, he showed his love every day.

She'd once lost everything she'd ever known and had died to the enjoyments life had to offer.

Akin had helped to heal her.

When her life had been threatened, he'd been there to save her.

Moving forward with him, she knew she'd always be loved, cherished, and protected.

THE END

OTHER BOOKS BY LOVE AFRICA PRESS

Bound Series by Kiru Taye

Bound to Fate

Bound to Ransom

Bound to Passion

Bound to Favor

Bound to Liberty

CONNECT WITH US

Facebook.com/LoveAfricaPress

Twitter.com/LoveAfricaPress

Instagram.com/LoveAfricaPress

www.loveafricapress.com